AP 100 days APRIL- OF MAY

April-May is back for another year at Trinity College, and she still hasn't changed her socks.

Sebastian, aka Edward, aka the boy with the lime-green eyes, is still drop-dead gorgeous and totally bad news. But then Fatty turns up. A giant of a boy who eats lamb-stew sandwiches and cries when no one's looking. And he's best friends with Sebastian. Awkward.

Juggling the evil teacher Mrs Ho as her new live-in mom, along with a new brother and a house with half a roof, April-May's life is as much of a mess as the crummy extension her dad Fluffy is building out back . . .

Praise for Edyth Bulbring

A Month with April-May

'The hectic pace of the dramas and April-May's own largely
benign view of them make this a fresh and entertaining novel
which reveals that teen trouble is the same the whole world
over.'
Julia Eccleshare, Lovereading4kids

'April-May is a feisty, frustrating, yet irresistible teenager with
a unique and very entertaining voice. Readers will enjoy
following her account of negotiating a new school and a new
family situation, learning the hard way that love and loyalty
may not always come in the ways you expect and that ulti-
mately the direction we take in life is our own responsibility.'
Booktrust

'I devoured the book in one sitting, but it passed the acid
test when my teenage daughter was seduced by Bulbring's
wit and humour, and was compelled by the sheer excellence
of the writing to keep reading.'
The Times (South Africa)

100 Days of April-May

'Hilarious . . . Edyth Bulbring has proved wildly popular, so
much so that her books are part of the syllabus for Grades
8 and 9 at a few schools [in South Africa].'
The Times (South Africa)

'Devoured in an evening and highly recommended.'
Media Update, South Africa

100 days of APRIL-MAY

EDYTH BULBRING

HOT
KEY
BOOKS

First published in Great Britain in 2013 by Hot Key Books
Northburgh House, 10 Northburgh Street, London EC1V 0AT

First published by Penguin South Africa in 2011

A CIP catalogue record for this book is available from the British Library.

ISBN: 978-1-4714-0051-3

1

Typeset by Palimpsest Book Production Limited, Falkirk, Stirlingshire
This book is typeset in Fairfield LH Light 11.25/17.25 pt

Printed and bound by Clays Ltd, St Ives Plc

Hot Key Books supports the Forest Stewardship Council (FSC), the leading
international forest certification organisation, and is committed to printing only
on Greenpeace-approved FSC-certified paper.

www.hotkeybooks.com

Hot Key Books is part of the Bonnier Publishing Group
www.bonnierpublishing.com

For Alistair, who was so awesome

The Eighth Story

There are only seven stories in the world, it is said.

You get the tragedy, where it all ends badly for the hero, the comedy, with a happy ending, and then there's the story where you take on a monster. You also have the tale about a voyage, where you leave as one person and return knowing a bit more about yourself, and the quest, where you find something or someone of great value. And then there's the rags-to-riches story, and, finally, the one about rebirth, where the central character finds a new reason for living.

But sometimes the story is a hodgepodge of all seven of these. It is the eighth story.

In my Grade Nine year at Trinity College I got caught up in a muddle of a tale. Tossed into this jumble were three people: a fat boy who ate himself silly because he felt worthless and angry, a kid who told lies because he was scared to face the truth and a useless shrink with a blind dog who couldn't help anyone because he didn't know how to help himself.

And then there was me – April-May February. Fourteen years old going on fifteen – the child of a divorced dad called Fluffy and a mom called Glorette. And my best friend, Melly, the girl who breathed through her mouth. And a golden boy with pale-green eyes called Sebastian, who made me stupid.

Our story could have ended any one of the seven ways that are set down for us. Or it could have had the other ending that goes with the eighth story.

In the beginning we didn't know how things would turn out. It all came down to the choices we made and the different roads we took towards our destiny.

In the end it all happened the way it did because of Melly, Fatty and me.

CROSSWORD CLUE 1 [four down]:
A boring or contemptible person or the foul
emission of wind.

One

The Big Fart

It's all Melly's fault. She's one hundred per cent to blame for landing me with Fatty. If she'd been around it wouldn't have happened. None of it.

It's the first day of my Grade Nine year at Trinity College. I am seated at the back of the classroom with my head buried in a crossword puzzle. The clue for six letters across is: *Missing*. I scribble *ABSENT* on the page and look at the seat next to me. It's empty. *VACANT*.

My best friend Melly is away this term. She's having an operation on her lungs at Groote Schuur Hospital in Cape Town to make her breathe like a normal person. She left yesterday, panting all over me through her mouth. 'Please don't mess up while I'm away, April-May. Try to keep your head down and your mouth shut,' Melly said.

I told her that I always keep my mouth shut – she's the one who can't breathe though her nose.

Melly presented me with a bracelet made from a piece

of leather and five ceramic beads which read: *WWMD?* (What Would Melly Do?). She says that if I'm ever in a tricky situation I must look at my wrist, pause, and consider my actions before leaping into boiling water. Melly's only been absent a day and I miss her badly. I feel *HOLLOW* (six letters).

Around me everyone's talking about their summer vacations. Plett and Umhlanga and Mauritius and Cape Town. And skiing in Austria. No one bothers to ask the bursary kid – that's me – what I did for the holidays, so I don't tell them that I was helping Fluffy with stock management at his travel agency.

Fluffy's my dad and he works at a funeral parlour called Swallows and Sons. He's in charge of the stock – what comes in, how long it stays and when it gets dispatched on its travels.

Controlling the stock takes a bit of juggling. Too much inventory creates space problems. Too little affects the end-of-the-month incentive bonus. And then there's the shelf life to consider. Fluffy says his clients are just like full-cream milk. If you don't keep a beady eye they'll go off and smell funny.

I toss the crossword puzzle aside and stand up as the teacher arrives. He introduces himself as Dr Gainsborough and then shouts, 'Sit!'

The class sits and so does a dog. It's a golden retriever

and it parks itself under the desk at Dr Gainsborough's feet. He says, 'Good girl!', and tells us that he is our homeroom teacher for the year. He also doubles as the Life Orientation teacher and the school psychologist. The Shrink. The person who deals with the crazy kids.

Dr Gainsborough then points to the dog at his feet. 'This is Emily,' he tells us.

Emily pricks up her ears and thumps her tail on the floor when she hears her name. Emily, it turns out, is blind. Dr Gainsborough hadn't known it when he picked her from a litter of seven SPCA puppies two years earlier. But when he discovered her visually challenged status it was too late to give her back – she was family. He pats Emily on the top of her head to reassure her of their kinship.

Dr Gainsborough takes out the register and calls our names. He soon gets to me, and I stand. 'So, this is you,' he says, as though recalling a fond memory. I tell him it is and he says, 'Fascinating. I've heard a lot about you.' He says this with a kindly glint in his eyes.

I've got a strange sort of celebrity status at Trinity College. I'm the girl who almost got expelled last year for attaching her tie to the school clock tower. And whose antics caused two pupils to nearly kill themselves by falling off the school roof, one of whom was my own dear Melly.

The other roof casualty was Sebastian, a boy with lime-green eyes who stole away from Trinity College soon after the incident, taking with him a slice of my cardiac muscle tissue.

I sit down and Dr Gainsborough comes to the end of the register. 'Ericca Ntona,' he says and looks up.

No one responds.

He tries again: 'Ericca Ntona.'

Dr Gainsborough is making an absent mark on the register when there's a knock at the door and the school secretary pokes her head into the classroom. 'So sorry to disturb,' she says. She's got a new kid with her. He arrived late and got a bit lost. She stands back from the doorway and the new kid walks into the room.

Walks is an understatement. He lumbers in, pulling his large body behind him. He is the biggest kid I have ever seen. He is about ten feet tall and ten feet wide with a face as dark and heavy as one of our famous Jozi summer thunderclouds. I can't take my eyes off this supersized kid.

There's a rude whistle from the middle of the room and Emily gives a little yelp. Whispers shoot across the room like sniper fire: 'lardass', 'jelly-belly', 'Buddha-butt', 'gross'. The mean kids toss words around the room like a bunch of delegates at a Crossword Puzzle Convention trying to determine the solution for *Obese insult*. They settle on a name: *FATTY* (five across). That's what he'll be called from now on. It is decided.

'This is Ericca Ntona,' the secretary says to Dr Gainsborough. 'The new bursary kid.'

Dr Gainsborough frowns at the secretary, looks down at his register and then up at Fatty. 'Ericca?' he says. 'It's Eric, surely?' He strokes the tips of his white goatee and peers uncertainly at Fatty through his pebble spectacles.

Fatty glowers and Dr Gainsborough swallows hard. 'Of course it's Ericca. And why not,' he says.

There are more sniggers from my classmates. 'Fatty, Fatty, Fatty,' they whisper.

I put my head down as the heat creeps up my neck. I know about dumb names. I'm April-May February. The calendar girl. But compared to Ericca Ntona, I got off lightly.

Dr Gainsborough looks around the classroom for a spare desk. I squeeze my thumbs in my fists until I hear the knuckles crack. *Not me, not me*, I beg the gods. *Please, not me*.

Dr Gainsborough points to the back of the classroom. At me. Fatty is going to be my new desk-mate for the term.

Come back, Melly, I yell inside my head. I'm getting landed with the fat boy with a mad-bad face and a girl's name.

Fatty barrels his way past the desks and throws his satchel down on the floor. Then he dumps himself into the chair next to me. As he settles, he lifts the desk two feet off the ground with his knees. I make myself as small as possible as he spreads his meaty arms across the desk.

Dr Gainsborough says that our lesson today will take the form of a short essay: 'My Family and Me'. He wants to know who we are. Get to know us, as it were. As he says this he reaches down under his desk and scratches Emily's ear.

I remember how weird I felt at the beginning of last year, coming to Trinity College on a bursary and not having any friends. I recall how Melly wheezed all over me within the first five minutes as she claimed me as her soul mate.

I take a deep breath in (not out), get out my exam pad and offer Fatty a sheet of paper. He reaches out. His hands are small; his fingers slender with nails as white as toothpaste. 'My name is April-May February,' I whisper.

Fatty looks at me and glares. He thinks I'm mocking him by making a stupid name joke. He drops his hand and turns away. I try and explain, but it comes out all wrong. It's hard to make clear to someone you've just met that your parents were at odds from the day you were born. That they liked different seasons and couldn't agree on which month to call me. I give up trying to set things straight and get on with my essay.

Fatty gets an asthma pump out of his blazer pocket and sucks on it hard. Then he gets an exam pad from his satchel. And a lunch box. While he writes he guzzles away at its contents: sandwiches like bricks filled with last night's stew.

I write my essay, ignoring the deep breathing and chomping going on next to me. I tell Dr Gainsborough all about my family. There's Fluffy, who is a stock control executive at a travel agency, and his best friend and intimate other, Julia Ho, who is the deputy principal at Trinity College. Then there is Just Sam Ho, Julia's eight-year-old son, who drives me mental most days but is also sort of okay. And last and best there's Melly, my special friend, who is more of a sister to me and who has problems in the respiratory department. That's my family. I stop there.

I doodle a bit on my desk and then I write my last sentences: *I have a birth mother called Glorette. She tells a lot of lies and is having a baby with her new husband, Sarel The Bloodsucker, in six months' time.* Enough said.

Fatty has finished the contents of his lunch box and makes a loud burp. The smell wafts over me. Lamb-stew and onions. Then he shuffles about and lifts a large buttock off the seat.

I know that move. A burp's one thing but there's no ways I'm standing for an almighty blast from the dark recesses of Fatty's large intestine.

I stand up. 'Don't you dare try and rip one near me, you fat pig,' I scream with the kind of lung capacity that Melly can only dream of. But as soon as the words are out of my mouth I want to shred my tongue and pickle it in shame.

Dr Gainsborough looks up and Emily starts howling. 'That is enough. Sit down!' His voice trembles with outrage.

I sit down, trying to keep my distance from Fatty, who has bowed his head and wrapped his arms around his chest. He is sucking on his asthma pump like he's never going to see another birthday.

The class hoots with laughter and peers around at Fatty and me as Dr Gainsborough gets up from his desk. 'Stay!' he commands Emily as he strides to the back of the classroom.

'I will not tolerate the shouting of insults in my personal space,' Dr Gainsborough barks, arriving in front of my desk and looking down at me with eyes that are no longer kindly. 'I will not have one student destabilising the emotional autonomy of another. Do you understand?'

I nod. Three nods. Which means I understand. And I feel really bad. About what I said.

Then Dr Gainsborough lifts the lunch box off my desk and frowns at me with eyes that tell me he thinks I'm some trouble-causing guzzler. 'Eating in class is against the rules.'

11

I swallow my tongue and wait for Fatty to own up. But he rasps in staccato time with my beating heart and says nothing. And lets me take the rap.

'Eating in class gets you an afternoon's detention. This afternoon. In my classroom. Straight after school. Do you understand?'

I nod. Four nods. Which means that I understand that Fatty has got me detention. On my first day. And I feel really mad. About what Fatty failed to fess up to.

'Finished your essay?' Dr Gainsborough asks me.

I give him my essay.

'Finished your essay?' he asks Fatty.

As Fatty tears the page out of his exam pad and hands it to Dr Gainsborough I catch a glimpse of a part of the line at the top of the page. It says: *I have no mother* . . .

Dr Gainsborough marches back to his desk and I look at my Melly bracelet. What Would Melly Do? My Melly would write the detention off as a little misunderstanding. She would become best friends (second best after me) with this sad, fat, hungry, silent, motherless orphan. She would breathe all over him and say, 'I can see that we are going to be the best of friends despite your antisocial habits.' That's what Melly would do.

I know Melly's way is the right way. The only way.

But I close my eyes to Melly's bracelet and lean over towards Fatty and say, 'You got me in trouble, you weasel.

I've got detention because of you. So from now on, dude, you just stay out of my way.'

Fatty says nothing, but I can see from the daggers drawn in the black holes of his eyes that he's got the message.

Soccer World Cup Update –
Days to Kick-off: 149

Match of the Day –
Fluffy and Julia Ho *vs* April-May

Two

Shacking Up

My father, Fluffy, and his intimate other, Julia Ho, are hunched over the kitchen table when I arrive at Chez Matchbox, the place I also call Home.

Fluffy is in a state of huge excitement. He is jabbing away at a piece of paper, scribbling and crossing out and adding up sums like a psychotic accountant after a double-espresso binge. 'I think I can just afford it,' he says as I walk in, mashing his huge tangle of hair into a billion knots.

'What can we just afford?' I ask him. Meat three times a week would be a nice start. Or the Interweb. And a computer to go with it.

He tells me that we're going to be doing some building. We are going to convert the garage into a bedroom and en suite bathroom.

I throw my arms around Fluffy's neck. How did he know? Number One on my wish list is to have my own private bathroom and not have to share bath scum with Fluffy. It's a dead tie with a computer. And the Interweb.

Fluffy says that he's also excited. In five months' time thousands of footie fans are going to descend on the country, looking for a place to call home for the duration of the Soccer World Cup. And Chez Matchbox, with its new en suite, will become this place for some homeless member of the European Community.

'Everyone's doing it,' Fluffy explains. South Africans everywhere are preparing to fleece the foreigners and make a killing on the back of the soccer madness. So why not him? If the euro holds up, the rent from the room will more than pay off the building costs and fund a holiday in Margate.

Mrs Ho is studying Fluffy's figures. 'This will mean a second bond. Is that wise, July? In this economic climate?'

What Mrs Ho means is Fluffy's economic climate. The one that he has been stuck in since he got retrenched from his newspaper job more than a year ago and began working in the dead people industry – first driving a tow truck for Willie's Wreckers and now working in a funeral parlour.

I hear the words second bond and I see *LOAN*. *ALBATROSS*. *DEBT*. Something Fluffy excels at getting himself into. Already his pay cheque barely touches sides. We can hardly meet the monthly payments on the one bond. A second bond is Bad News, and I tell Fluffy precisely this using these two words.

Fluffy says that I must think positive. People should have the confidence to make their own luck. In return I tell Fluffy that I think affirming thoughts about our bond and my destiny all the time. Every month I send karmic blessings to the Governor of the Reserve Bank, trying to make her drop the interest rate. A percentage point drop means a tiny stash of cash for the Rainy-day Tin. A rise means two-minute noodles for the month.

Mrs Ho places a cautious hand on Fluffy's arm. 'July, can we talk about this? I have a few thoughts.'

Fluffy glances up and catches the look on Mrs Ho's face. It's an expression that he has learned to read during the past year that they have been steady intimates. It means that she wants to talk to him in private.

Fluffy tells me to go and do my homework. I reply that I finished it all during my afternoon's detention and that he's not to worry, I'm happy to hang out with him and Mrs Ho and chat.

Mrs Ho's eyebrows leap into her hairline like angry question marks. 'Detention?' she queries.

Fluffy punishes his hair. 'Detention!' he exclaims.

I bite my tongue in two and say that I think I should go and clean the bathroom. And tidy my room. And tidy Fluffy's bedroom too.

Fluffy says, 'Oh no you don't, young lady, sit down.' And they subject me to verbal waterboarding until I explain how Fatty's (I call him Ericca Ntona) antisocial habits caused me to express myself in a loud and emotionally incontinent manner. Yes, I called the new bursary kid a fat pig.

Fluffy and Mrs Ho give me looks full of reproach. Looks I can read because I have known Fluffy for nearly fifteen years, and Mrs Ho for more than one year, which is long enough for me to know her 'I'm so, so disappointed in you, April-May' look.

I tell them that they've got me wrong. I'm a chubby chum. I love fleshy people. There's Ishmael – Fluffy's best friend next to Mrs Ho – who drives a tow truck for Willie's Wreckers. He's got more shares in the blubber department than an obese whale, and I like him just as well as thin people. And I am also inordinately fond of pigs, who are the cleanest animals on Planet Earth, even though they will eat just about anything and make bad smells. Like Ericca Ntona (Fatty).

I start backing out of the kitchen before I stuff both feet into my mouth, leaving the two of them shaking their heads.

In my bedroom I find Sam Ho lolling on my bed. He's fiddling with my cellphone and listening to my music on my iPod. An open bottle of nail varnish on my bedside

18

table next to a half-painted wooden toy is proof that he's been in my cupboards. Again.

He doesn't see me enter the bedroom. Nor does he see me pull the duvet from under him, an action which dumps him on the floor. I grab my stuff and drag him by one ankle towards the door and chuck him out.

There are two things worth mentioning about Sam Ho. The first is that he belongs to Mrs Ho. The second thing is that while I think he's okay for an eight-year-old troll, mostly he's an annoying brat who should stay out my room.

Sam Ho hobbles down the passage towards the kitchen, squealing like a stuck pig – a stuck goat. I make a mental memo to ban the pig word from my daily discourse. It's a three-lettered stink bomb.

Sam Ho is hobbling because he hurt his back in a car accident some time ago. It caused the loss of a family member – his father – and damaged his spine. He was on crutches for most of last year and is still learning to adjust to putting one foot in front of the other instead of swinging and swaying on crutches.

He is also hobbling because it is guaranteed to score sympathy points with Fluffy and get me in trouble for beating up on him.

I follow Sam Ho towards the kitchen – intent on damage limitation – and catch the tail-end of the conversation.

'Moving in with April and me would make us a real family.'
Then there's a pause and I conclude from the slobbery
silence that Fluffy and Mrs Ho are having a romantic
moment across the tomato sauce.

Which Sam Ho and I put a very sharp stop to with our
appearance.

Mrs Ho tells Sam Ho to hush, please, love, stop
squealing because we are having an adult confab about
some life-changing issues.

'If Julia moves in with us,' Fluffy explains, 'then she
could rent out her house.'

The cash would help Fluffy pay off the building loan,
and the two of them would recoup the damage and split
the huge profits on his rent-the-en-suite-to-affluent-
soccer-tourist scheme.

Fluffy is flushed. He looks like he's won the Lotto.

'But where would she sleep?' I make squiggly eyebrows
in Mrs Ho's direction. Somebody's got to ask the question.
And I'm still smarting over them chewing my ear off about
Fatty. I'm not going to make things too easy for them.

Chez Matchbox boasts two bedrooms. One is Fluffy's
and the other is mine. Fluffy flushes some more. Then
he blushes over his flushes while Mrs Ho starts shredding
her cuticles.

'Of course Julia will share my bedroom with me,' Fluffy
finally says.

20

I'm a grown up sort of a girl with a mind as broad as Fatty's butt. I know all about the facts of life and the physical goings on between two people who have declared themselves in love and are committed to an intimate partnership. 'Of course she will,' I say to Fluffy. 'But where will Sam Ho stay if you rent out his house?'

Twenty minutes later I am storming down the road in the direction of Melly's house with a satchel containing most of my worldly possessions. Sam Ho to share a bedroom with me? Is that where the thinking is going? Is that what Fluffy means by of course Sam Ho will live with us? I'd prefer to share a bedroom with a pig. Or Fatty.

I'm halfway to Melly's house when I remember that she's not there. She's in Cape Town, having her lung butchered to help her breathe like a normal person. I backtrack to the park across the road from my school. It's a favourite hang-out of mine.

A couple of kids are on the see-saw, so I head for the trampoline. I jump high. So high that I can see over the palisade fence, across the road and into the school soccer field.

Some kids are kicking a couple of soccer balls around. The goalie is totally rubbish. He's sitting on the grass in front of the goalposts with his head in his hands. And as the balls hit him, he hunches over as if he is trying to protect himself rather than save the ball. Lazy old thing.

Then I see that the kids are using the lazy goalie as a target. And the harder the balls hit the bowed figure, the louder they laugh.

Call me a nosy parker, or meddlesome or even a snoop, but there is one thing I can't abide, and that's bullies.

'Hey! Stop that!' I shout, and then I quit jumping and get my satchel. My cellphone has thirty text messages but I don't bother to read them because I know it's just Fluffy saying *Please, come home, April. Please, come home so we can talk.*

I run out of the park and head towards the school sports fields. I peer through the fence and watch as the mean kids continue slamming those balls at the crouching figure on the grass.

Then, before I can shout stop right away else I'll come over and kick those soccer balls into the backs of your throats, the stooped figure gets up. The kids jeer and whistle and a couple of the scaredy-cats start running away. This makes me smile wide. Run, you cowardly custards. Run, you yellow-bellied bullies, run. I laugh as they run.

Then I recognise the goalie. It's Fatty. He lumbers towards the side of the field, his head down, wheezing. And then he looks up and sees me. Standing there laughing. And I can see from the dark expression that crosses his face that he thinks I'm part of this mean game. And that I've been watching and laughing all this time while the other kids jeered and beat up on him.

CROSSWORD CLUE 2 *[three across]*:

A common animal with four legs or to follow someone closely in a way that annoys them.

Three

The Big Lie

Fluffy and me are not communicating this morning.

'Please, hurry up, April, I've got to get to work early today. I'm expecting a huge delivery.' He checks his cell-phone again and shakes his head in disbelief. 'Twenty.'

I eat my toast, slowly. Small bites and long chews. Then I pack my lunch box with the speed of a sloth on Valium. But before I can brush and floss each one of my thirty-two teeth seven times, Fluffy pushes me out of the front door and into our family transport.

Fluffy gets to take home one of the company cars every day. An employee perk. And if I had to choose between the tow truck from Willie's Wreckers that Fluffy got to drive last year, and the hearse from Swallows and Sons, I would choose the stiff-mobile every time – it's a lot more roomy. Plus the air con is top notch to ensure maximum client comfort.

I check the back of the stiff-mobile for stowaways

(Fluffy sometimes brings his work home) and then get in the front.

On the way to school Fluffy tries to engage me by talking about the stock delivery of twenty items he's been warned to expect at Swallows and Sons this morning. It's a conundrum. There've been no freak accidents this week, he says. No train smashes or extended family massacres.

Not yet, I want to tell him, Sam Ho hasn't moved into my bedroom yet.

'And there were certainly no pile-ups on the freeway yesterday,' Fluffy goes on. Ishmael, his pal from Willie's Wreckers, would have told him if there had been any serious bloodletting on the roads.

I refuse to take the bait. I will not be drawn by Fluffy on the riddle of the twenty pieces of merchandise that will be waiting for him in his in-tray when he gets to work. I turn up the volume on my iPod and stare out of the window.

'He's going to sleep in the lounge,' Fluffy finally says, but I don't hear him until he yanks the headphones from my ears and says it again. Slow and loud into my right auditory cavity. 'Sam. Ho. Is. Not. Going. To. Share. Your. Bedroom.'

I tell Fluffy that he hasn't thought of multiple deaths from claustrophobia and suffocation. It happens when too many people are shoved into a confined space and don't get enough oxygen.

Fluffy says that I must pull myself together. 'This is

our chance to be a real family,' he says. And after the soccer I'll get the bedroom with en suite bathroom. And Mrs Ho is bringing her television set along with her PVR. And her washing machine.

I tell Fluffy in that case I suspect a flood. Casualties as a result of too much water in the summer is always a safe bet in Jozi.

Fluffy beams at me and says that this would probably explain the consignment of twenty. And would I tell Sam Ho that he will be picking him up after school as Mrs Ho is stuck in meetings all afternoon?

'For sure I will,' I say.

I make it to class as the first lesson bell stops ringing. The seat at the back of the class is empty. And so is the seat in the front of the class. No Dr Gainsborough, no visually impaired Emily and no Fatty.

The class descends into anarchy for ten minutes until the deputy principal and my future housemate Mrs Ho arrives and says we must calm down immediately. 'Dr Gainsborough is having a meeting with one of the parents,' she says. 'And I'll be supervising the class until he returns.' Then she points a finger at me and says Dr Gainsborough would like to see me in his private office. Her face tells me not to ask why. But just go. Now.

The door to Dr Gainsborough's office is shut. Emily is lying across the entrance and when I try and knock she gives my hand a vicious tongue-lashing. I let her drool on my hand a bit and tell her she's a nice dog and that I taste better than I look, so she's not missing out on too much.

The door opens and Dr Gainsborough says, 'Out the way, girl.'

Emily and me get the idea that he wants both of us to move, so we make way for Dr Gainsborough and Fatty and a woman as pale and thin as Fatty is large and dark.

'Five minutes to see your mom to her car and then back to class, Ericca,' Dr Gainsborough says.

Your mom. That's what he said. I heard it right. I know sixty-five per cent of the world's teen population is going deaf from excessive iPod usage but I'm not one of them. I only got my iPod last year, and as much as I try and overuse it to make up for thirteen years of auditory drought, I still can't seem to get deaf. Dr Gainsborough definitely said 'your mom'. I ponder the words in Fatty's essay which I spied yesterday: *I have no mother* . . . And then I ponder the big riddle of genetics as Fatty and the thin paleface walk away. That is until Dr Gainsborough tells me crisply to please come in and sit down.

I get a tight feeling across my tummy. I may be a lot of things but there is one thing I am not: I am not a rat. I don't tattle on my peers. I'm not a telltale tit. Dr Gainsborough just has to ask me one question about the bullying on the soccer field yesterday and I will claim to have been as visually impaired as his dog.

I sit down and Emily parks herself at my feet as Dr Gainsborough pulls out the essay I wrote in class. He pushes his glasses to the top of his nose with his thumb and peers at me.

Dr Gainsborough says he found my perspective on My Family and Me 'interesting'. I tell Dr Gainsborough in that case he will probably be interested in the latest installment and I proceed to update him. I tell him my father's love interest and her eight-year-old troll-child are moving in with their television and PVR.

Dr Gainsborough interrupts me between the couch in the lounge and the washing machine and says that what interests him most about the essay on My Family and Me is the two sentences about my mother.

I try to recall what I wrote yesterday, distracted as I was by Fatty scoffing his way through the contents of his lunch box. *What the heck did I write?* I am beset by lamb-stew-and-onion-induced dementia and draw a blank.

No worries. Dr Gainsborough gives a knowing smile and reads the interesting two sentences to me: 'I have a birth mother called Glorette. She tells a lot of lies and is having a baby with her new husband, Sarel The Bloodsucker, in six months' time.'

I tell Dr Gainsborough I have to, have to go to the

bathroom to attend to a delicate feminine hygiene matter. I get up from my seat. Emily gets up too and licks me softly on the hand. 'I want to see you twice a week, April-May. I think you need to talk to someone about your mother issues,' Dr Gainsborough says as I make it to the door. He looks at me with kindly eyes as I close the door and run.

I get home after school to find Fluffy pacing in the kitchen. His face is as bleached as Fatty's melanin-deficient mother. He is too pale for a coloured sort of a person. He says: 'Where is he?'

'Where is who?' I ask.

Fluffy says this is no time for jokes, April. 'Sam Ho wasn't waiting for me after school. He's missing. Do you know where he is?'

He looks over my shoulder with a hopeful face as though Sam Ho might be right behind me and then breaks into a sweaty smile. 'Oh, there he is,' he says. Then his face changes and he starts yelling. 'Where the heck were you?' he shouts at Sam Ho. And, 'I waited for an hour.' And, 'I was going out of my mind with worry.' And stuff like that.

Sam Ho just stands there while Fluffy makes noise. And then there is a sharp bark and a hairy missile launches itself at Sam Ho.

I once again ponder the big riddle of genetics as I examine the creature. He is, Fluffy tells us, the progeny of a Great Dane, the Apollo of breeds, and a dachshund, also known as the sausage dog. He's like a hairy log on stilts.

Nameless Dog, Fluffy tells us, is the survivor of a tragic family drowning. He raises an eyebrow at me. Death by excess water – my prediction was spot on this morning.

It is a sad story and Sam Ho and me are as silent as two graveyards as Fluffy tells it to us while we try and stop Nameless Dog from chewing bits off our fingers.

Fluffy relates how Nameless Dog arrived at Swallows and Sons that morning in the company of twenty other creatures almost identical to him (Nameless Dog, not Fluffy). Except, all twenty were no longer breathing.

Apparently Nameless Dog and his nineteen brother and sister puppies decided to take a bath in their owner's swimming pool yesterday afternoon. Except they couldn't swim. When their owner – Miss Geraldine Frankel – returned from her game of bridge, she found nineteen sopping-wet bodies laid out neatly – and stiffly – by the side of the pool. And a sopping-wet Nameless Dog, nestled between the paws of an exhausted and soon-to-be-deceased Hotdog (Nameless Dog's mother). 'It was clear that Hotdog had spent every ounce of energy trying to save her pups,' Fluffy says. 'Then she perished, leaving behind one little orphan.'

Fluffy also says that Miss Frankel is a loyal patron of Swallows and Sons and is insisting that Hotdog and Co get buried in the Frankel family plot.

'But what about the orphan?' I ask him. The orphan who is chewing a hole through my iPod.

The little survivor, Fluffy says, will be with us for a while. Miss Frankel is in the process of selling her house with the killer swimming pool and in the meantime is staying in a hotel which forbids all animals except fish (which can swim). As soon as she has bought a new house, with a tennis court and no swimming pool, she will reclaim the orphan puppy and give him a name.

Sam Ho starts sniffing. And his eyes are red. There are four words for what is ailing him: Allergic to Nameless Dog. Fluffy looks at him with concern and then remembers. 'Where the heck were you after school? I waited and waited . . .' Then Fluffy squints at me: 'You did tell him like I asked?'

I assure Fluffy that I wrote Sam Ho a note telling him to meet Fluffy at the gate after school and put it in his locker. Just like he'd told me.

Then Fluffy looks at Sam Ho, who says, 'No.' This is not true. There was no note. Not in his locker. 'April-May is lying.'

I tell Sam Ho that he's a lying brat. And Sam Ho says that I'm a lying brat. And we 'lying brat' away at each other until Fluffy says just hold on a moment, the note was obviously overlooked. There's just been a mix-up. 'Now hold your tongues.'

Sam Ho glares at me and I glower back at him. His face is red and the tips of his ears and his dumpling nose are throbbing like beacons. Both of us know that there was no mix-up. And that one of us is a lying brat.

Soccer World Cup Update –
Days to Kick-off: 128

Match of the Day –
April-May *vs* Mom

Four

Mom Issues

I am lying in the shade of the sour-sour tree in the back garden of Chez Matchbox when my cellphone rings. I check the caller ID and reject the call. Someone out there is hell-bent on driving me crazier than I already am. In the last five minutes I've had three calls from the same number. The caller is a person of no words. Just loud breathing.

Thirty seconds later my cellphone bleeps. I have a text message: *Answr ur fone. It's me. Melly.*

It's been three weeks since term started and my best friend Melly jetted off to the hospital on the coast to have an operation to make her breathe like a normal person. I can't wait to talk to her. We've been out of contact since Melly's mom decided she should have peace and quiet away from 'bad influences' (aka me) as she prepared for the big op, and then some more peace and quiet during her recovery. To secure this outcome Melly's mom kidnapped The Goddess.

Melly has a BlackBerry. It is the goddess of all cell-phones. In contrast I have a phone that looks like a brick that was born when the idea of building the ark was just a faint twinkle in Noah's eye.

The Brick rings and I answer. 'Melly?'

There is the sound of panting in my ear. Then a small voice says, 'April-May?'

Melly tells me that she's called three times before and I've put the phone down on her. 'Yes, I did,' I tell her. 'I thought you were a stalker.'

Melly says she's calling from her father's cellphone as The Goddess is still being held hostage. She says that she's been dying to tell me about her operation. I tell her that I'm dying to hear. So Melly tells me.

The surgeons have carved and patched her lung, ampu-tated several adenoidal obstacles in her nasal passages, excavated a million clogged taste buds, and she is now a certified nose-breathing, smelling, tasting person.

She breathes into the phone. Can I tell the difference? Can I hear that she is breathing at me through her nose?

I tell her she sounds like a phone stalker.

Melly says, 'Please, April-May.'

I can hear how important it is to her, so I tell her that she sounds like the most regular nose-breathing person I have ever heard. Then she breathes through her mouth at me and while it sounds exactly the same I tell her the difference is remarkable. And it's as clear as crystal that she has graduated to the race of nose-breathers with flying colours.

Melly fills me in on her life as a regular nose-breather. Three days after the operation she could smell. Did I know that some people's armpits smelled like garlic? And two days after that she could taste. For the first time in her fourteen years on Planet Earth she tasted broccoli. It is disgusting – why hadn't I told her?

Since the recent acquisition of functioning taste buds she's been eating polony sandwiches morning, noon and night. 'Polony sandwiches are my favourite food. Just like you, April-May.'

Then Melly asks about my life. She says that she's dying to know.

I tell Melly that I am now a certified crazy person along with nine other nutcases at school. We have all been sentenced to therapy sessions with Dr Gainsborough twice a week. There are ten crazies. Two per grade. The minimum quota to justify the cost of having a shrinkage service at Trinity College.

Melly gasps. She says that I must be mad. There's nothing crazy about me. Why am I seeing the school shrink?

I tell Melly that I have issues. Mom issues.

'But, April-May, all girls have mom issues. It's the natural order,' Melly rasps at me. And then a cross voice which I recognise as belonging to Melly's mom says, 'What do you think you are doing on your father's phone? Give me that at once. You're supposed to be resting.'

I hear the sound of tussling and gasping as Melly and her mom deal with their issues. Melly's mom wins.

'Is that you, April-May February?' The voice over the phone is cross. Melly's mom is not as fond of me as she could be. She says my family has vulgar transportation habits and I'm a bad influence on Melly.

'It is I, your favourite calendar girl,' I tell Melly's mom.

Melly's mom snorts. 'Melanie is not supposed to speak at all. Not for another two weeks. And she must not get excited. She is in a very delicate stage of recovery.' Then she puts the phone down without saying as much as have a lovely day, April-May February, and give my regards to your father.

I think Melly's mom has vulgar telephone habits. I had been on the point of telling Melly about my sessions with Dr Gainsborough in his private office (which doubles as the Nutbox twice a week). I would have told her that I get shrunk in the session before the new bursary kid – Ericca Ntona (Fatty) – and just after a sad Grade Ten girl who has issues about swallowing her tongue.

Melly doesn't know anything about Fatty and I would have told her everything. Right from Day One, when he got me detention. And I would have also told her about

Nameless Dog, who has been expressing his trauma at being orphaned by chewing his way through the contents of our house 24/7, and who is lying next to me under the sour-sour tree, snacking on Sam Ho's favourite Lego man.

But if Melly's mom hadn't been the one to cut our conversation short, my mom would have. Because she has arrived and is peering down at me. Just as I'm about to continue reading my new library book.

So I read. Because I do not wish to speak to her. And she shouldn't be here. It's not her weekend to have me.

'What are you reading, May?' Mom asks.

Mom calls me May, Fluffy calls me April. When they split up two years ago they split the assets and my name. Some people take divorce a bit literally.

I roll my eyes and lift up the book. She can read the title for herself, can't she?

'*The Interpretation of Dreams* by Sigmund Feud.' She reads it slowly.

'Freud, not Feud,' I snap. Talk about a Freudian slip.

'Is it interesting?'

'No, Mum, I'm reading it because it's boring.'

'May, would you put that book down. I want to talk to you.' Mom speaks to me in a timid sort of a voice. It makes me want to make her cry.

I give a large Melly-like sigh, as though I'm giving my under-used nasal cavities some physiotherapy. 'What?' I glance up. My eyes cross over as I try and look at Mom without seeing her. I can't look at her face in case she catches my eye. I can't look at her body because . . . I just can't. My eyes start to feel funny, so I focus on her mouth. Her mouth makes words that say, 'Sarel and I were just in the neighbourhood . . .'

My mom works for a public relations company, which means that she lies for a living. And she just can't seem to leave her work at the office on the weekends. Sarel and Mom are never just in the neighbourhood, unless they're intent on bugging me.

Sarel is my mother's new husband. He is a blood-sucking lawyer from Pretoria and he is ninety-two per cent bald. To compensate for his premature hair loss, Sarel wears a wig.

'. . . so we thought we would just pop by to see whether you've changed your mind?'

I don't say anything. For a spin doctor who spends her working days twisting and tweaking the facts for fat-cat corporates, she should be more precise. Changed my mind about what? I give her my cross-eyed blank look.

Mom sighs. 'If you have decided to come and see the scan of your new sibling with Sarel and me?'

'No,' I say. And I start texting randomly on The Brick.

Mom sighs again. 'No, you haven't decided, or no, you don't want to?'

Nameless Dog lifts his head from Sam Ho's mangled piece of Lego and growls. And then his fur rises like a fan of quills on his back.

Before I can say hey, Nameless Dog, this guy's a big-shot leech from Pretoria, he'll sue the hide off you if you so much as touch a hair on his head, Nameless Dog leaps into the air. He flies in the direction of Sarel, who has just appeared at the back door of the house.

The next fifteen seconds are a blur. When Sarel emerges from the vortex of activity he is wigless and there is no sign of Nameless Dog. 'What was that?' Sarel asks, rubbing his hand tenderly across the top of his head. His head which looks like a pincushion.

'Sarel, what is that?' Mom asks, looking at Sarel's head, and at his face which has collapsed into a mottled red blob.

It transpires that Pincushion-head has been having secret hair transplants in preparation for the best day of their lives – for when Baby is born. Sarel wants to be the kind of dad his child can be proud of. A dad with a full head of hairy pincushion hair.

Mom and Sarel forget about me and have an emotional moment. And then they remember me and ask if I've decided if I'm coming with them to the hospital to see a 3D movie of the person who will mark the best day of their lives.

I say, 'Yes, and it's no.' They can keep their baby scan and their hair implants and I'll keep home with Sigmund Freud and Nameless Dog, who is busy burying Sarel's wig in a sunny spot by the washing line.

'What's his name?' asks Sarel.

Nameless Dog looks at me expectantly, ears pricked. I could tell Sarel that he doesn't have a name because Miss Frankel is going to christen him when she claims him and takes him to his new home without a killer swimming pool. But I decide otherwise. I have a genetic disposition towards untruths. 'His name is Killer.'

Nameless Dog howls in appreciation of my choice and then snarls at Sarel and Mom – to prove his credentials.

Sarel puts an arm around Mom's waist. I look away. From that waist.

Mom shudders. 'I wouldn't want a dog like that. It's vicious. You should get rid of it, May.'

I glare at Mom.

'What's wrong, May? What did I say?' Mom says, catching my icy stare. She shakes her head at me, like my behaviour is some sort of divine mystery. 'I just don't know what has gotten into you these past couple of months. You're impossible and that's the truth.'

Bingo. Mom is looking at me like she's going to cry.

I pick up *The Interpretation of Dreams* by Dr Sigmund Freud and start reading.

Mom and Sarel leave, Mom gulping her way out of the yard like a sad fish chucked out of its bowl of water. Sarel like he really hopes the scan shows a son and not a daughter.

I don't tell Mom that I've got her number. I know the truth. I know that she has lied to me from the day I was born.

CROSSWORD CLUE 3 [six down]:
A state of extreme confusion and disorder or
a pejorative term for a nuthouse.

Five

The Big Day

Today is B-Day. The day of the Builders, the Big Move, Bathing and Bedlam. In that order. I swallow a fist of Fluffy's vitamin B-complex tablets to give me some zip.

Today the builders, Trevor and Phineus, start tearing the garage apart to make it into a groovy pad for some first-world soccer nut, who will pay through the nose in euro-gold for living in Chez Matchbox's luxury suite. And then vacate said groovy pad after the final whistle has been blown, leaving it all to me.

Trevor and Phineus are builders we can trust not to rip us off with shoddy work and long lunch breaks. They are trustworthy because they are related to Ishmael, Fluffy's best friend, through a brother on his late father's side of the family. They are close relatives. 'Very close,' Ishmael has assured Fluffy.

It is close on eight o'clock and we've been waiting and waiting and the builders still aren't close to pitching up.

They are an hour late already and are making me late for school and Fluffy late for work.

Fluffy says, 'No worries.' He'll whisk me off to school in the stiff-mobile and then whisk home again to meet the builders. Swallows and Sons don't sweat an hour here or there – most of the clients aren't in a big rush to go anywhere.

Today is also the big move. It is the day that Mrs Ho and Sam Ho vacate their modest home in the suburbs and move into Chez Matchbox to cement our two half-families into one united family unit.

Fluffy has liberated some shelf space in his cupboards and set his softest pillow on the right-hand side of the bed next to the window for his new roomie, Julia Ho. Meanwhile I have spent the past month fostering in Nameless Dog an overwhelming love for the couch where Sam Ho will be attempting to lay his head every night. One of them is going to have to make a bed on the floor.

Fluffy whisks me off to school humming like a piece of rancid cheese and tapping madly to the violin concerto that plays non-stop in the stiff-mobile. The music is intended to keep the clients at peace on the journey to their final destination. It makes me want to impale my eardrums on the sharp ends of the windscreen wipers.

Fluffy says, 'Isn't this great?' Tonight he gets to come home not just to me, but to Sam Ho and to Julia – just like a regular family. 'Life doesn't get any better than this,' Fluffy says.

'And Nameless Dog,' I add.

Fluffy nods. 'Yes, and the dog.' The dog that Fluffy had told Julia would be happily ensconced with Miss Frankel in her new home with the tennis court by the time the big move happened. Because Sam Ho has allergies to all canine hair – and to Nameless Dog's hair in particular.

'No stress, it's just for five months.' We'll survive until the soccer madness comes to an end and Julia and Sam Ho go back to their cottage in the 'burbs, I console Fluffy. 'Then it will be just the two of us again. Back to normal.'

'Five months?' Fluffy stops tapping. 'Well, April, if things work out we could be looking at a more permanent arrangement.' He stares straight ahead, determined not to catch my eye. 'I don't want to rush things,' Fluffy says and screeches to a halt outside the school gates.

I am struck dumb. I slam out of the stiff-mobile and rush off to class. I've missed the first lesson, but I'm just in time for Physical Education.

Physical Education is two capitalised words for the equivalent of having hot needles thrust into my eyeballs. It is the third B of my B-Day – bathing. Which is one word. Hell.

Don't get me wrong, I like swimming. I love flopping about in Melly's swimming pool. I adore lapping in the

47

bath at Chez Matchbox, or seeing how long I can hold my breath underwater in Melly's jacuzzi. Aquatic sports are my forte. For sure I'm a big fan of swimming. But not at Trinity College.

I grab my swimming kit from my locker and make it to the changing rooms, where Tiffney and Britney and all the girls in the mean-girl gang are busy telling Coach that they can't swim today: 'It's that time of the month.'

Coach is a middle-aged man with three daughters of his own. He likes chatting to Britney and Tiffney and Courtney and Stephney (and all the other girls with names stolen from American television soaps) about their time of the month as much as he likes talking to his own daughters about it. Which is not much at all.

He mutters something about them all bleeding to death with all these times of the months happening week in, week out, and then he asks if anyone will actually be swimming today.

There are some hard-core Charlene Wittstock clones, and the boys, standing at the diving-board end of the pool flexing their pecs. Then there's Fatty. And me.

Coach says get into pairs. 'Take it in turns and practise the life-saving drill.' He'll be away for five minutes, getting the schedule for the gala (having a quick smoke).

Everyone pairs off. Everyone except Fatty. And me.

I've been labelled a million and one things by the

48

mean-girl gang at Trinity College. I am: 'Flat-chest', 'Skinny-butt', 'Bursary Kid', 'Polony-muncher', 'Brainbox', 'Smelly Melly's Pelly', 'The Freak Who Arrives At School In The Dead People's Car'. But over the past four weeks I have grown a new label: Fatty's Swimming Buddy.

Fatty and me haven't been big on dialogue since I called him a physically challenged porcine animal on the first day of school. And since he saw me watching him getting bullied on the soccer field and laughing. We only converse with each other on a strictly need-to-talk basis. And when we do address each other, we both pretend to be deaf and invisible.

I tell Fatty that he can go first. Fatty gives me his I-don't-see-or-hear-you look, so I say, 'Okay, I'll go first then.'

I run and leap into the swimming pool and swim out into the middle. Then I wait for Fatty to jump in and displace thirty per cent of the over-chlorinated swimming pool water, accompanied by loud cheers and clapping from the bleeding monkeys watching at the side of the pool.

Fatty strikes out doggy-paddle-style in my direction. He's not a big fan of aquatic sports – he can't swim much.

I assume the in-distress drowning position, which involves a lot of arm-waving and head underwater-bobbing until I feel Fatty grab me by the hair and haul me to the side of the pool.

I'm going to skip the description of the next part of the

life-saving exercise. It can be viewed on YouTube. It goes under the label: *Fat boy and skinny girl drown each other in hysterically funny life-saving exercise*. It has been viewed more than thirteen thousand times and has been liked more times on Facebook than *Ugly girl with pimples asks jock on a date*.

For this slice of fame I have Britney and her BlackBerry to thank. And Fatty for being such a lousy swimmer and seven times my size, so that it is impossible for me to save him from drowning without us both swallowing the remainder of the over-chlorinated water in the swimming pool.

I'm not insecure. I don't need votes of public approval from my peers. YouTube is for losers with too much bandwidth on their hands and nowhere for their fingers to go.

And what I definitely don't need is two hours of detention from Coach for messing around and showing off in the swimming pool and imperilling the school's swimming safety record. Thanks, Swimming Buddy.

B-Day only gets worse. In the second lesson after break I am assigned crazy-girl status and excused from Religious Instruction to have my bedlam appointment – my therapy session with Dr Gainsborough to deal with my mom issues.

I am prepared for my shrink today. I have lined up three dreams that I can report to Dr Gainsborough and

I have a good joke about a Freudian slip. I like to make these sessions meaningful for Dr Gainsborough, who is a slavish Freudian (right down to his goatee and funny round spectacles). Lined up on the shelves in his office between two identical busts of Dr Sigmund Freud are *The Interpretation of Dreams, Jokes and Their Relation to the Unconscious* and thirteen other books by the great psychoanalyst himself.

And lined up in front of Dr Gainsborough's desk is Emily, who blindly wags her tail as I enter, and Mom, who does not wag her tail because she does not have one and is not blind either.

I see Mom and I mean to say, 'Hi, Mom, what a lovely surprise,' or something to that effect. But what I really say is, 'What are you doing here, you liar?' Which is a Freudian slip. Except it's not a joke – and it's not funny.

I'm going to skip the next hour in the office with Mom and Dr Gainsborough. It's not on YouTube because the sessions with Dr Gainsborough are bound by patient-shrink confidentiality and I am not obliged to share my sessions with Britney and her BlackBerry. But if it was on YouTube it would be labelled: *Crazy girl spends hour staring at floor while blind dog licks her hand and shrink shares meaningful looks with mom.* It's a long title and it wouldn't get lots of likes on Facebook.

When I get home after my two-hour detention with

Coach (cleaning last season's gob out of the school's goggles and snorkels) the house is very quiet. Quiet like the inside of the big freezer at Swallows and Sons, where Fluffy sometimes stores our perishables when the electricity at Chez Matchbox is cut off. There is no sign of Sam Ho. And there is no sign of Nameless Dog – just a pile of shredded Grade Twelve Biology essays piled up on the dog-hair-covered couch.

Fluffy and Mrs Ho are staring at each other across the kitchen table. They are not playing the blink first game.

'This has been one of the worst days of my life, July,' Mrs Ho says, breaking the silence.

Fluffy is clawing at his hair. 'I'm so sorry. Today of all days. I wanted everything to be perfect. Forgive me, Julia. I'm so, so sorry.'

Mrs Ho reaches over and grabs Fluffy's hand, trying to stop him beating up on that hair of his. Then they see me and look up; their eyes glassy.

'What's happened?' I ask. The sense of tragedy is marked on their faces. 'The electricity been cut off again?'

They shake their heads. It's worse than that.

Fluffy's hand hits that scrubby patch of hair again. 'It's Sam Ho. He's in hospital. I nearly killed Sam Ho.'

Soccer World Cup Update –
Days to Kick-off: 102

Match of the Day –
April-May *vs* Fatty

Six

Dumb Chop

There's a seriously wicked game going on among my feathery friends in heaven. And I'm not talking about the angels. It's the birds.

This is how the game works: every bird gets a certain number of points for hitting a particular target. And the first bird to get a thousand points wins. I know about this game because of the stiff-mobile. It is Exhibit A. Proof that the Aves species of Johannesburg are engaged in a fiercely competitive game of Target.

I'm betting that hitting the Swallows and Sons vehicle gets a bird five hundred points, which makes it an über-popular target. If you hit it twice in one day, you double up on points in record time and win. Which, in turn, means that every evening before supper Fluffy has to clean the stiff-mobile. 'It's all about respect,' Fluffy says. His clients deserve to be carried to their final destination in a vehicle that has been scrubbed of starling guano.

After the car is spotless, Fluffy puts it away in the garage so that he can start out the fresh day in a fresh car with a fresh client.

This is the car that Fluffy, Mrs Ho and me are piled into. Except Fluffy hasn't got around to cleaning it yet – because of the Sam Ho crisis. We are heading off to the hospital with a fruit basket (a couple of naartjies and a banana), some board games and a change of clothes for Sam Ho.

On the way to the hospital Mrs Ho fills me in on the day's drama. It sounds like way more fun than cleaning green goop out of aquatic apparatus for Coach.

Fluffy had fetched Sam Ho from school and brought him home to a house covered in dust – from the building – and canine hair – from Nameless Dog. Predictably, Sam Ho's eyes swelled into blood-red orbs, his chest closed up (making him sound like a sixty-Texan-Plain-a-day Hospice inmate) and his skin broke out in a leprous rash.

'Your father did what he thought best,' Mrs Ho says.

In the interest of restoring Sam Ho to health, and to avoid the wrath of Mrs Ho, Fluffy had turned to drugs. 'It was just a couple of antihistamine. They're over-the-counter too. People eat them like Smarties in the autumn,' Fluffy says.

But instead of a couple of antihistamine, Sam Ho had chowed down on Fluffy's old bronchitis tablets.

'He's allergic to penicillin,' I say, bringing the dramatic Sam Ho saga to its conclusion.

55

'He's allergic to penicillin,' Mrs Ho says, like an echo. And then she turns to Fluffy and shakes her head. 'I just can't imagine why Sam took the wrong tablets.'

I tell Fluffy and Mrs Ho that I'm so glad Sam Ho's going to be okay and Fluffy beams at me like he's a one-hundred-watt bulb and says, 'That's my girl.'

Call me sentimental or schmaltzy, but I like Sam Ho fit and healthy. There's no joy in tormenting a dead kid.

Sam Ho is in a ward with five other kids who look in far worse shape than he does – he's bouncing about on his hospital bed as if it's a trampoline.

Mrs Ho and Fluffy fuss over Sam Ho like he's had a near-death experience while I set up a game of snakes and ladders. Sam Ho is a genius at the game and in our last tournament he beat me nineteen times in a row. I figure I should take advantage of his weakened condition to stage a comeback.

Sam Ho rolls the dice and I roll the dice, and I climb those ladders and fall down those snakes, but Sam Ho rolls and climbs and climbs. He climbs those ladders through whatever ceiling it is that prevents eight-year-old trolls from succeeding until the score is five–nil.

'Well done, son,' Fluffy says and he puts a fatherly hand on one of Sam Ho's shoulders as Mrs Ho puts her motherly hand on the other.

The picture of Father, Son and Mrs Ho fills my heart

with venom. 'So, how come you made such a stupid mistake with the pills?' I ask Sam Ho. I say these words in the tone that the first snake of Creation used with Eve when he offered her the apple and promised to be her friend for the rest of eternity. But Sam Ho knows I'm calling him a dumb chop by my use of the 'stupid' word. Which he is.

A strange expression crosses Sam Ho's face. It's the same look he gives the dice before he rolls. He knows he's risking a score that will take him shooting down a snake to the bottom row of numbers, but he doesn't have any option but to play. 'I didn't make any mistake. I took the pills from the box on the shelf. From the box Fluffy told me to,' Sam Ho says.

There's a sharp gasp from the side of the bed. The kind of sound that some poor aunty makes when you turn off her life-support system. It's Mrs Ho. 'July?' she says.

Fluffy shoots panicky looks between Mrs Ho and Sam Ho and me. He shakes his head. 'I told you to take a couple of Allergex. The box is on the top shelf in the bathroom. Clearly marked. Next to my bronchitis muti – but I told you to make sure you took the Allergex.'

Sam Ho shakes his head back at Fluffy. And as much as Fluffy splutters and mutters and says, 'That's not how it happened, Sam Ho, it isn't . . .' Sam Ho just shakes his head at him. 'I took two pills from the only box on the shelf.' Then Sam Ho says he's feeling kind of wiped out and senses a relapse coming on. He needs to rest. He's been booked in overnight for just in case.

Mrs Ho feels Sam Ho's head. 'I don't like the look of him,' she tells Fluffy.

I tell Sam Ho that I don't like the look of him either. His face is the stiff mask of a liar and I don't like it one bit.

On the way out of the hospital Mrs Ho says she wants to stop by the hospital pharmacy to get some Allergex, 'because it seems we have none in the house'. She says this in a tight-lipped sort of way which makes Fluffy look miserable and grab at his hair.

Fluffy and me hang around outside the pharmacy while Mrs Ho goes inside. Five minutes later she emerges with the drugs that will keep Sam Ho's eyeballs from exploding and discourage him from ripping layers of skin off his face. 'You'll never guess who I met in the pharmacy,' Mrs Ho says.

I don't even have time to play the guessing game with Mrs Ho because Fatty and his pale-faced mom emerge from right behind her.

There are some people called Determinists who believe that there are no coincidences in the world. Everything that happens can be related to a prior incident or association, no matter how big or small. And maybe they are right because the chance meeting at the pharmacy of Fatty, his mom and Mrs Ho turns out to be all my fault.

'He was involved in a bullying incident at school and had an asthma attack,' Mrs Ho whispers to Fluffy.

Fluffy looks sharply at Fatty. 'Serves him right,' he hisses back at Mrs Ho. 'A boy that big can really hurt the smaller kids.'

Mrs Ho pulls Fluffy into a corner and fills him in the way Grace – Fatty's mom – had filled her in: some malicious student at Trinity College had attempted to drown Fatty in swimming class. 'The poor kid is a novice swimmer and had a terrible asthma attack after school.' That's why they're here – getting another asthma pump for Fatty.

'The other boy must have been big,' Fluffy says and gives a long whistle through his teeth.

The other boy tells Fluffy and Mrs Ho it's time to make tracks. 'I've got loads of homework to do.' (That I didn't get to do because of Detention.) I don't say the last part. It only causes tension in the home.

But before I can make my escape, Mrs Ho introduces Fluffy to Grace, and Fatty to Fluffy, and Grace to me. 'You and Ericca obviously know each other?' Mrs Ho says.

Fatty and me grunt at each other and I fix my eyes on his and wait for him to blow me out of the water for attempting to submerge him permanently in the school swimming pool. I hold his gaze and dare him to rat me out. And as I stare into those big brown eyes that tell me he dislikes me as much as I dislike him, I see my face. Just for a second. And then Fatty blinks and I'm gone.

And then we are all on our way home. Fatty and pale-faced Grace in their shiny red Toyota Corolla and Fluffy, Mrs Ho and me in the stiff-mobile, which is displaying yet another special gift from the starlings and their pals the Indian Mynas on Mrs Ho's side of the windscreen.

Mrs Ho tells Fluffy all about 'the Ericca Ntona matter' for thirteen of the fifteen blocks home. It turns out that Fatty was found abandoned as a baby in a locker room and after being in and out of foster homes for fourteen years has now been formally adopted by Grace. However, things are not going very well because Fatty is a difficult, distrustful child and has bonding issues, which is why he is seeing the school shrink.

Mrs Ho knows all this stuff because she's the one who interviewed Fatty when he applied for a bursary at Trinity College. 'He's enormously bright,' Mrs Ho says.

'Yes, enormous,' Fluffy replies.

Mrs Ho says that it breaks her heart to see the way Fatty and Grace interact. 'Did you see the body language? That boy is as stiff as a gurney around that lovely woman. He's determined not to show her an inch of affection.'

'Not an inch,' Fluffy murmurs.

We get home and Fluffy parks the stiff-mobile in the

street – the garage is off limits because of the builders. We all take a good long look at the hole Trevor and Phineus have bashed in one side of the garage wall.

'They don't seem to have made much headway. Just a lot of mess,' Mrs Ho says, which scores her one hundred per cent for observation. It's Ground Zero.

'They say it will be all over in a couple of weeks, Julia,' Fluffy replies in a croaky voice, the one he uses when the words get stuck in his throat because he's not sure if they're going to leap out of his mouth and call him a liar.

Nameless Dog has left a welcome-to-Chez-Matchbox present for Mrs Ho in the entrance hall which she obligingly tramples all the way down the passage into the kitchen. He has also expressed his opinion on the woollen sweater Mrs Ho knitted Fluffy for his birthday last year (seventeen scraps strewn across the kitchen floor). And he has given a short review of Mrs Ho's new library book (it's in three parts and missing the cover).

'This has not been a good start to our new life together, July,' Mrs Ho says before she collapses onto the couch, which has been reupholstered in hair by Nameless Dog.

I make a quick retreat to the bathroom and leave Fluffy to deal with Mrs Ho's emotional meltdown. Inside, I give the toilet a loud and vigorous flush and run some water to block out the heartfelt sounds from the hairy couch. Then I open the bathroom cupboard. There are two boxes on the top shelf. The first contains tablets clearly marked Allergex. The other has a faded label.

I flash back to the hospital and to Sam Ho's face. The face with the shut doors and drawn blinds. There are three possible explanations for Sam Ho's behaviour: either Fluffy tried to kill Sam Ho, or Sam Ho is a dumb chop – or Sam Ho was trying to kill himself.

CROSSWORD CLUE 4 [five down]:
An act of starting play in field hockey (in which two opponents strike each other's sticks three times and then go for the ball) or a person who uses strength or influence to harm or intimidate those who are weaker.

Seven

The Game

I call Melly on her cellphone, but The Goddess is sulking. She clicks off without allowing me to leave Melly a message. I try Melly's dad's phone, which isn't sulking, and tells me to 'go away, you ruddy nuisance' in Melly's dad's voice.

When cellular communication spits in your eye, it's time to go back to the Stone Age. I deploy my initiative and call the Groote Schuur Hospital switchboard. Then I demonstrate my get up and go and tell the matron on duty in Ward Seven that it is absolutely imperative that I speak with Melanie.

The matron demonstrates her go-away-and-get-lost zeal and says, 'Why? This isn't a hotel, it's a hospital. Are you a blood relative?'

I tell Matron that I am closer than a blood relative to Melanie. I am Mara Louw from M-Net *Idols* and I am phoning Melanie to congratulate her on being one of the one thousand lucky contestants who will be auditioning live on television in three weeks' time. It is totally essential for the show's ratings and for Melanie's future as the country's favourite pop idol that I speak to her.

Thanks to Mrs Ho and her television set and her PVR, which have taken up residence at Chez Matchbox in front of the couch, I am now one hundred per cent au fait with reality shows. *Who Wants to be a Millionaire?*, *Survivor*, *Big Brother*, *Idols*, you name it. I am a certified reality show addict.

Matron says sorry, Mara, but Melanie is going to have to take a rain check on fame and fortune. 'She hasn't been doing too well, and as we speak she is in theatre undergoing a second operation.' Then Matron says in a gentler voice, 'Are you a young lady called April-May February from Johannesburg?'

I say, 'How did you guess?'

Matron says Melanie had told her all about me. 'She hoped you would call and I'm sorry to have to give you this bad news, April-May. Call this evening and I'll be able to tell you how she is.' *Click.* (The click is Matron putting down the phone.)

I assume the lotus position and perform ten minutes of Buddhist breathing exercises to stop my heart from exploding. Five hundred and fifty-two. Breathe out. Five hundred and fifty-three. Breathe in. Then I concentrate on the actual breath without counting. And finally I focus only on the spot where the breath enters and leaves the nostrils, which is sort of the upper lip area.

By the end of ten minutes my heart rate is back to a normal person's heart rate and not someone who is terrified that she is going to lose her best friend on the operating table in Groote Schuur Hospital.

This is my second session of meditation for the day. The first session takes place at school in the privacy of the Lost Property Room following an incident that causes my heart rate to mimic that of an Olympic athlete on dodgy vitamins. It's the reason I was calling Melly in the first place.

If I had been able to speak to Melly I would have told her all about Fatty and the Triple-T game. The game that Britney and Stephney and Tiffney played with Fatty at first break which caused my heart to palpitate.

The two lessons before first break are Maths. Call me a calculator if you like, but for sure I devour numbers and logarithms and equations the way Fatty guzzles lamb-stew sandwiches.

And Fatty has emerged as a bit of a number-cruncher himself. I have a fifty per cent chance of walking home with the Maths prize this year – Fatty holds the other fifty per cent. It's why we are the bursary kids. We get to beat all the dumb kids who pay fees to come to this school.

My Maths teacher this year is Mr Benjamin Bendell and he is crazy about everything and anything mathematical. Ben-squared is particularly obsessed with fractals, which a French super-genius by the name of Benoit Mandelbrot developed to explain patterns in the seemingly random shapes around us.

A whole cauliflower can be seen in every cauliflower floret – this is one of Mr Mandelbrot's more incisive claims. It's not my favourite vegetable, but I get the logic.

And Ben-squared has taken Mr Mandelbrot's thesis further – in every naartjie pip there is a citrus orchard. In every lamb chop, a flock of sheep. In every Catholic priest, the Vatican. And so on. He has plotted the Mandelbrot set (a mathematical set of points in the complex plane, the boundary of which forms a fractal) in a PowerPoint presentation. For the next two hours he shows the class slide after slide of visually represented fractals. We see seahorses and naartjie peels and paisley-shaped bunches of broccoli.

It is complex maths and Fatty and me appear to be the only two students who have some grasp of what Ben-squared is on about. The rest of the class have a virtual mini-riot, Tweeting and Facebooking and MXiting on their cellphones.

The bell rings and I make my way to the quad to eat my lunch. My lunch box reveals a lettuce-and-tuna sandwich on wholewheat bread. There is also a banana and some freshly squeezed granadilla juice.

The pattern that is developing from the daily content of my lunch box is clear. Mrs Ho is waging war on Fluffy and my tardy dietary habits, which have flourished like a fungus in the absence of a sensible hand on the refrigerator.

In the three weeks that she has been living at Chez Matchbox, polony and two-minute noodles have been banished from the shopping list. A balanced diet and regular exercise are the keys to a healthy mind and body, Mrs Ho says.

My tongue is busy doing press-ups in my mouth, digging granadilla pips out of my underdeveloped wisdom teeth, when I hear the chant. It's coming from the soccer field, where the up-to-no-good kids take their nonsense (far away from the eyes and ears of the stop-this-nonsense-immediately teachers).

The chant gets louder. And out of the random noise, a pattern takes shape. 'Tell the truth. Tell the truth. Tell the truth.'

By the time I get to the top field a lynching party has gathered. Twenty kids have formed a circle on the field. There are the usual suspects: Britney, Stephney, Tiffney and the rest of the mean-girl gang. There are also a couple of arbitrary guys who like to hang with mean girls. And at the centre of the circle is Fatty.

There are a few things that I have learned in my almost fifteen years on Planet Earth. The first is that people don't get what they deserve: bad guys get away with murder and live. Good people get cancer and die. The second is that if you put bubblegum in your hair you're going to have to cut it out with a pair of scissors (along with half your hair). And the third is that there are moments in your life that you will wish you could do over. Things you know you could have done better, or said better, or where you could have been better. This is one of those times.

I stand at the edge of the circle and I watch Britney and Stephney and Tiffney scream at Fatty. 'Tell the truth: What size pants do you wear?', 'Tell the truth: How much do you weigh?', 'Tell the truth: How many sandwiches do you eat every day?' The questions come at him like bullets.

They shout and laugh and scream at Fatty, who sits in the middle of the circle with his hands over his ears. He doesn't look at them. He doesn't answer them. And he doesn't give them all a knuckle sandwich to make them shut up.

I know I have to do something, so I stick my elbows out and I walk into the crowd the way Fluffy says I should walk if I'm ever in a situation where my personal space is threatened. 'Those elbows will make people move,' Fluffy says.

Fluffy's always got his finger on the ebb and flow of the pulse of life. It's in his job description.

The crowd of mean girls moves as I walk with my elbows. They move towards me and into my personal space. Their faces are so close to me that I can count the number of blackheads on Tiffney's nose and the tiny dark hairs on the top of Britney's lip.

They push me into the circle, so that I am standing next to Fatty's crouched form. And then they play the 'tell the truth' game with me.

They shout things at me phrased as questions that are meant to make me feel like a flat-chested, polony-sandwich-guzzling bursary kid who gets a ride to school in the dead people's car. I'm all of these things. And I've heard it all a million times. The mean-girl gang has never scored high on originality: 'What car does your dad drive?', 'What bra size do you wear?', 'Who pays your school fees?'.

If we were on *The Weakest Link* I would have walked off with the jackpot, but it's not that sort of a game and I can feel the circle of kids closing in on me. I need to get away. To get some air. To breathe. White dots are dancing at the back of my eyes, forming a pattern in which I slowly recognise two words: Walk Away.

I do the elbow walk through the crowd again. As I walk away I hear them start on Fatty for a second time: 'Tell the truth. Tell the truth. Tell the truth.'

I walk away from the mean-girl circle and find some silence in the Lost Property Room with the manky socks and the spare shoes and the lunch boxes of forgotten cheese sandwiches.

I breathe and breathe until I can't hear the chants in my head any more. Then I get my satchel and cut school. I run from that red-brick building with its blind clock tower that tells me that people like Fatty and me will never belong. I go home and sit on the couch with Nameless Dog. We watch reruns of *Big Brother* and *Idols* and *Survivor* and *The Weakest Link*. And none of it seems very real.

Before I go to bed I phone Groote Schuur Hospital and speak to a cross nurse in Ward Seven. She says that information about Melanie can only be divulged to family members and she knows for a fact that I am not Mara Louw, nor am I Melanie's mother, because Melanie's mother is sitting outside the intensive care ward. *Click.*

There is another thing that I have learned in my short time in this world. This other thing is that if my friend Melly had been on the soccer field she wouldn't have stood by and watched Fatty being bullied. No. She would have shouted out for it to stop with all the breath in her chopped-up little lungs. But she couldn't, because she's lying in intensive care. And I didn't. I walked away and

71

left him. I know that by taking that walk of shame I am guilty of being the weakest link.

And I'm not sure who I hate more for making me a coward. The mean-girl gang, Fatty or me.

Soccer World Cup Update –
Days to Kick-off: 55

Match of the Day –
Fluffy *vs* The Builders

Eight

Dodgy Dreams

Fluffy says he's exhausted. He's been having problems falling asleep of late, and when he does finally drop off he has bad dreams.

I ask him what he's dreaming about.

Fluffy says it's the same dream. He's running. Someone or something is chasing him. But as he runs, his feet get heavier and heavier. Then they get sucked into a muddy bog – or is it cement? And he can't move his feet any more. He's frozen to the spot. He wakes up just as someone or something catches him.

I tell Fluffy that his dream is possibly the second most unoriginal dream since the falling-off-a-tall-building-and-waking-up-just-before-you-hit-the-ground dream. It's text-book Freud.

Fluffy says, 'But what does it all mean, April?'

I tell Fluffy that he's running away from something and he is terrified of getting caught – which is the textbook Freudian explanation for the run-away dream.

Fluffy says, 'Ah, yes, Julia and Sam are going out for the morning.'

I can see that Fluffy is still in denial. Still running in the hope of getting away. It's not who is going out this morning, it's who is coming in. 'It's the showdown with the builders today,' I say gently, and watch Fluffy's face collapse into a puddle of tired lines as he feels the concrete sucking away at his ankles.

The builders are having a crisis meeting with Fluffy and Ishmael at Chez Matchbox this morning. The first item on the agenda is: Progress on en suite. The second item on the agenda is: Lack of progress on en suite. The third item on the agenda is: What has happened to the advance payment for labour and building materials that Fluffy laid out at the start of the job?

After nearly two months the garage area still resembles Ground Zero. It has occurred to me (and perhaps to Mrs Ho, whose lips have gotten thinner by the week) that all the builders do each week is move the pile of rubble about.

Fluffy has pulled Ishmael into the meeting to try and sort things out before Mrs Ho takes matters into her own hands – like wrapping them around the builders' necks and wringing the life out of them.

It is common knowledge among relationship experts

that there are several things that cause stress in an inti-mate friendship. In particular, the experts and me have identified: moving house, building renovations, a badly behaved dog and the dirty-sock-and-wet-towel habit prac-tised by eighty-two per cent of the male species (of which Fluffy's dirty-sock habit is a subset).

The wet-towel habit requires said man-slob to leave a wet towel on the floor/bed/any place other than on the designated towel rack. This is usually coupled with the dirty-sock habit, which involves balling a dirty pair of socks together, necessitating the washer of socks (Mrs Ho) to stick her fingers into the fecund depths to unball them before shoving them into the washing machine. 'It's a nasty little habit,' Mrs Ho says. And when she says this she looks at Fluffy as though he's her nasty little habit. One that she wants to kick.

Between the big move, the builders, Nameless Dog and the dirty-sock habit, things have become a bit strained between Fluffy and Mrs Ho. Understatement.

Ishmael says Fluffy mustn't stress. The meeting with the builders will put everyone back on the straight and narrow. Fluffy mustn't forget that Trevor and Phineus can be trusted because they are members of his family on his late father's brother's side.

Fluffy looks at his watch and says, 'Trevor and Phineus are an hour late, but we can't start the meeting without them, can we?' Ishmael says, 'No, we can't.' So they drink a couple of pots of rooibos tea while they wait.

Two hours later Mrs Ho and Sam Ho return from the shops and then go straight back out again. Mrs Ho says that she's not getting involved in 'this mess' and the further she can be from the builders the safer they will be. And will Fluffy put the groceries away, please. She says, 'Please.' Full stop. But she means please don't let me come back and find the groceries still in their packets on the floor where I left them.

Another hour passes and then the doorbell rings. Ishmael answers the door and shouts to Fluffy that there's a bloke at the door asking for him. Is he expecting another visitor apart from the builders this morning?

Fluffy goes to the door to look and says, 'No, this is Trevor, your relative – on your late father's brother's side of the family. You gave me his contact details when I decided to convert the garage.'

Ishmael makes big eyes at Trevor and lets him in.

Trevor says that Phineus sends his apologies but he is in the middle of something.

'How could he do this to me? This is important. It's not a game,' Fluffy says. He looks at Trevor as though he is facing down a nightmare.

Trevor says that's precisely what it is. Phineus is in the middle of a game of blackjack at Gold Reef City Casino and his chips are down. Until he makes back his stake and the losses from yesterday and several days before yesterday he can't leave.

It's a bad start to the meeting and things get worse. Fluffy offers Trevor some tea, but Trevor looks at his watch and says, 'Somewhere in the world it's cocktail hour . . .' and that he thinks he could do with something a little stronger.

Ishmael says he thinks Trevor has been drinking cocktails for the past three hours because he smells like he has been gargling with brandy. 'And in any case we don't drink hard liquor in our family,' Ishmael says, giving Trevor a glare full of meaning.

Trevor lifts his sunglasses and gives Ishmael a bloody eyeball and says that his family were suckled on hard liquor, and what did Ishmael say his family name was again?

Now that I look at Trevor and Ishmael I see that they don't look at all alike. They can't possibly be related. And then Ishmael looks at Trevor and I think he comes to the very same conclusion, because Ishmael takes Fluffy aside and says, 'I think I've made a big mess.'

I can't bear to watch Fluffy shred his hair so I go and sit on the couch and write a letter to Melly. My dear friend Melly, who is slowly on the mend at Groote Schuur Hospital following her second operation.

I have been instructed by Melly's mom that Melly must not be upset or excited in any way, so I only tell her about the unseasonable weather (violent thunderstorms) and some of Nameless Dog's antics (only the ones that will not cause undue stress – obviously).

Nameless Dog is sitting on the couch next to me, chewing away at some supermarket bags as he watches reruns of *The Dog Whisperer*, an excellent educational show that teaches owners how to train their dogs and wean them off their unsociable habits. Fluffy says that if there is one thing we can do to try and keep a bit of peace, it is getting Nameless Dog to stop devouring everything in sight. 'It's driving Julia mental.' (A bit like me, though Fluffy tries not to use any of the crazy words in reference to me in case it stops me dealing with my mom issues in therapy with Dr Gainsborough.)

So in the interests of harmony I get Nameless Dog to watch *The Dog Whisperer* twice a day. And Nameless Dog learns from dog-training guru Cesar Millan (and his pit bulls, Daddy and Junior) respect for the territorial rights of the alpha species (humans). I'm just telling Melly how Nameless Dog tenderised Mrs Ho's leather briefcase (a graduation present from her deceased husband) when I hear the front door give a vicious slam. And then a car roars off, with a screeching of tyres.

I go into the kitchen and find Ishmael and Fluffy

doubled up. Tears are streaming down Fluffy's face and Ishmael is snorting like a farmyard animal whose name I have forbidden myself from using in the English form (*Sus domestica*).

'What's the joke?'

So Fluffy tells me. It turns out that not only are Trevor and Phineus not related to Ishmael at all – and they have never even met before today – but, in fact, Trevor and Phineus are not even really builders. 'Can you believe it, April – not even builders!' Fluffy cackles.

I tell Fluffy that I can believe it. 'They are just a couple of chancers who saw you coming,' I say.

'Well, at least that explains why they didn't do much building. I mean, knocking a hole through a wall and shifting the rubble about isn't really building, is it?'

I tell Fluffy it certainly isn't. And as it is now only eight weeks until our euro-flush soccer-mad guest arrives to take up residence in Chez Matchbox's garage, perhaps he should find a couple of people who actually build for a living.

Fluffy and Ishmael laugh a bit more and say things like 'You fool!', 'You idiot!', 'You klutz!' and 'Oh, what a mess!'. Then Mrs Ho comes home and Fluffy and Ishmael stop laughing.

'What happened to the advance payment for labour and building materials that you laid out at the start of the job?' Mrs Ho asks Fluffy. This was item three on the agenda. The item Fluffy and Ishmael didn't get around to asking Trevor about before he had to rush off to quench his thirst.

Fluffy says no stress and calls Trevor. The cellphone goes *click*. He phones the number again. It goes *click*. Again. Fluffy does this a couple more times and gets the *click* response.

Mrs Ho looks in the fridge and sees a gaping wound that requires deep prodding with a rusty nail. She says, 'And what happened to the groceries I brought home and asked you to please pack away?' She looks around the kitchen and the lounge and spots Nameless Dog, who is sitting on the couch with his nose still in a stash of super-market bags, with one eye fixed on *The Dog Whisperer*.

Cesar Millan is holding a bowl of food at waist height and will not set it down until Junior sits. 'Dogs must be given permission to eat,' Guru Cesar says.

Then Mrs Ho says things like 'That blinking dog! For goodness' sake, July, all those groceries!' and 'Couldn't you just do one little thing!' and 'This is just the last straw!' Then she storms off to the bedroom shouting about last straws and absolute limits and slams the door.

Sam Ho peers into the kitchen and says, 'What's all the noise about?'

I tell him that Fluffy's been ripped off by the builders

– they've taken all his cash and run. And that Nameless Dog has eaten all the groceries. And that his mother says it's the last straw and has gone to rage in the bedroom.

Sam Ho says that it all sounds like a bad dream, and I tell him that Freud would agree.

Fluffy gives me a look which says, lie to me, April, please, just one small little fib. And then he says, 'You think the builders aren't going to repay the deposit? My cash is all gone?'

I tell Fluffy that I can't lie to him (on this matter). What hasn't already been lost on blackjack at Gold Reef City Casino is being poured straight into the bottlestore as we speak.

Ishmael pulls a chair out for Fluffy, who sits down and stares over at the couch in the lounge. 'Ruddy dog,' he whispers.

He looks towards the bedroom door. It is shut very firmly. And then it opens and Fluffy's eyes light up in hope.

Mrs Ho stands in the doorway with her hands bunched at her sides. Her face is a picture of wrath. She throws a fist out in the air and a pair of Fluffy's dirty balled-up socks sail into the room. And then she throws out her other fist, which holds a soggy towel – evidence of another filthy habit to which Fluffy is falling prey. 'I've had enough! And this *is* the last straw!' Mrs Ho points at the soggy towel and then walks out of the front door.

CROSSWORD CLUE 5 *[seven across]*:
*A good deal or an agreement in which two people
or groups each promise to do something.*

Nine

The Gods

Nameless Dog and me leave Fluffy and Ishmael staring in wretched silence at each other across the kitchen table and slip off to the park.

On the way I allow Nameless Dog to snack on some garbage bags – one must learn never to put one's domestic waste out on the pavement for the rubbish truck until morning – and to file his teeth on a few car tyres – one must learn always to park one's car in a garage (unless it's being converted into a bedroom with en suite bathroom for a wealthy soccer-mad tourist).

The park is deserted apart from a couple of tramps sleeping off their liquid lunch under the plane trees. I tie Nameless Dog to the pole by the swings and lie down on the merry-go-round and stare at the sky.

I think of Fluffy – alone again without Mrs Ho as his intimate friend. I think of Chez Matchbox without Mrs

Ho. I think of Fluffy and me in Chez Matchbox without Mrs Ho. A wave of misery breaks over me.

Call me soppy or cheesy or even soft, but life at Chez Matchbox without Mrs Ho would be an unhappy space for Fluffy and me. I can't bear for her to go. Who will wash my clothes? Who will scrub the dirty pots? Who will cook suppers of which the main ingredient is not two-minute noodles? And the deal breaker – how will I watch *Idols* and *Big Brother* and *Survivor* without Mrs Ho's television and PVR?

I know I am not a victim. I have the power to turn things around. I can take charge of my own destiny. I close my eyes, hold my thumbs in my fists as hard as I can and start bargaining with the gods.

The trick to bargaining with the gods is not to give too much away in the first round – to always have something in your back pocket to break any potential stalemate and clinch the deal. Five minutes into the first round of bargaining with the gods I am down to being cordial to Sam Ho and Sarel The Leech. In return, the gods will ensure that Fluffy and Mrs Ho patch things up and she will stay at Chez Matchbox to wash Fluffy's rancid socks and clean the pots and allow me to nourish my addiction to reality shows.

I wait for a sign from the gods that my offer has been

accepted. One of the tramps under the trees howls in his sleep. It is an angry howl. I interpret this as a thumbs-down from the gods. They want more.

I throw in Mom. It will be tough on me, but I can convert from cold antagonism to hot civility. It is time to change tactics in my conflict with Mom in any case. But I don't let the gods know this.

Nameless Dog gives a growl and a whimper from his spot by the swings.

'What more do you want, gods?' I whisper, opening my eyes and gazing up at the sky. A sharp breeze is playing with the clouds. I see a whale. It grows a trunk and is transformed into an elephant. And then its trunk is squashed into its face and becomes a snout. A curly tail attaches itself to its hind quarters. It takes on the guise of a farmyard animal with an insatiable appetite for lamb-stew sandwiches.

The animal hovers above me in the sky and I close my eyes. I don't need Dr Benoit Mandelbrot or Ben-squared to interpret the pattern that is emerging from these random cloud shapes. The gods want their pound of flesh. They want me to cease my cold war with Fatty.

I resist for a good five minutes. But in the interest of Fluffy's happiness and in pursuit of my own domestic comforts I finally make my pact with the gods. I will suspend hostilities with Fatty and Sam Ho and Sarel – and limit my aggression towards Mom to covert sabotage. It is done.

Music fills my ears. The gods are serenading me. Yes, they are.

I sit up and look around. Nameless Dog is straining at his leash, trying his best to reach a discarded Kentucky Fried Chicken packet. And in the far corner of the park, under the one plane tree that has not been colonised by sleepy tramps, are two figures. Singing.

Call me a gullible fool, an idiot or just simply crazy (the crazy word is gaining currency), but in the dimming light of this Jozi autumn afternoon, I see the gods.

I drag Nameless Dog away from his early evening snack and together we make our way towards the two gods sitting under the plane tree. They have their backs to me but it appears that one is playing the guitar. Both are singing.

The gods sense my approach and stop singing. The guitar-player turns around. The dappled sunlight casts a golden glow on his features (which are indeed godlike), features which I recognise and for which I have a certain psychotic fondness. Like I have a fondness for heights and rough waves and huge thunderstorms and sour sweets that make my cheeks collapse and my ears hurt. Things that are bad for me.

'Hey, Bella,' the god says.

'Hey, Bas,' I say and try and shift the golf ball which has lodged itself in my windpipe.

Sebastian gets up and reaches out his palm. I wipe my palm with his. Almost. We don't touch, but I feel the heat.

'Long time, Bella,' Sebastian says. Understatement.

Sebastian calls me Bella. It's the name I would have called myself if I'd had the choice and not been held hostage to the whims of two unseasonable and discordant parents. The last time I saw him was more than a year ago – as he tumbled down from the roof of Trinity College. It was the disastrous end to a crazy escapade that nearly got me expelled and caused my friend Melly to get concussion and sprain her ankle.

'How's the leg?'

'Legs,' Sebastian says with mournful glee. The fall from Trinity College's roof rewarded him with a shattered thigh bone in one leg and a broken ankle in the other.

'I limp. I think I'll limp for the rest of my life.'

'Cool,' I say.

'Yeah, I find release from my pain through my music.'

'Cool,' I say. Then I smack myself in the face because I sound like a linguistically challenged person (Britney or Tiffney or Stephney).

'Meet the other member of my band,' Sebastian says.

The other member of Sebastian's band emerges from the shadows and I nearly choke on my golf ball. It's Fatty.

He is no god. And his face is dark with dislike at the sight in front of him – that's me.

I see the gods are testing me.

'Hey,' I say to Fatty. And I look at him properly, so that his shape attaches itself to my cornea. I see him for the first time in more than three months.

'Hey,' says Fatty, and he looks back at me like he is also seeing me for the first time – which is a bit weird because as far as I know he hasn't made any blood-pacts with the gods.

I suck in my chest and summon all my cordial powers. 'I heard you singing. You have a good voice.' Realising 'good voice' might show a lack of commitment to the pact I reboot the expression on my face, retune my vocal cords and add, 'Magical.'

Nameless Dog agrees. He leaps into Fatty's lap and buries his nose in his trouser pockets. After a lot of tussling and snuffling he emerges with a sandwich. Fatty allows Nameless Dog to run away with his sandwich to the safe spot by the swings.

'What's the dog's name?' Fatty asks.

I catch Sebastian staring at Fatty and me with his pale-green eyes. But mostly he is staring at me. I want to say, ah, stop staring at me like that, you make me feel shy, but the golf ball does its thing in my throat and I make a sound like, 'Ahhhhsssstttostaaare . . .'

'Alistair? Did you say Alistair?' Fatty says. 'It means "protector". That's an awesome name for a dog. Alistair The Awesome-ist. It suits him.'

When I hear Fatty's speaking voice I realise that it's the first time I've really heard it. It's not a big voice to match his size. Or like his singing voice which is warm and solemn. It's small and gentle and cracked.

Nameless Dog returns and sits at Fatty's feet. He does not chew them or sniff them or try and use the takkie laces as dental floss; he just closes his eyes like he's discovered his slice of heaven.

'This is the awesome-ist dog I have ever met,' Fatty says.

'He's mine,' I say, but I pull my mouth into a smile and give the word mine a gentle lilt at the end, just in case the gods are listening. I tell Fatty that Nameless Dog is a compulsive eater and uses food to self-soothe as he had a very tragic childhood and feels worthless and angry.

Fatty nods and says, 'I know how he feels.' And then he scratches Nameless Dog on his tummy.

Sebastian is still staring at me, so I stare back and find myself drowning in his eyes. He asks me how Trinity College is doing and I say that as he can see it's still standing – which is very lame and I am so wishing that he would stop staring at me because everything that comes out of my mouth is stupid and dumb and irrational (and cruel evidence that Sebastian still has a kinky effect on me).

I ask Sebastian how he likes boarding school (dumb question) and he says that it's just school, but his parents are glad that they got him out of Trinity College and away from the bad influence that caused him to injure himself in a madcap escapade. And then he laughs, his mouth wide, showing the gap between his front teeth, and I laugh too, because it's a noise I can make with my mouth without sounding dumb. Except I give a horrible whistling snort at the end.

I tell Sebastian that I'll be off home then – otherwise I'll have to hang myself from the plane tree with Nameless Dog's leash – and he says he'll Inbox me on Facebook or catch me on MXit. I say, 'Of course.' Except that I know he won't because I don't have a computer and The Brick does not do anything other than calling and texting.

And Sebastian says that if we want to move from the virtual to the physical he always hangs out in the park on the weekends when he's home from boarding school.

I click my fingers at Nameless Dog and he looks at me with one eye and then carries on pretending to snooze. I *click-click* with my tongue and Nameless Dog closes the opened eye and gives a good imitation of snoring.

'Hey, Alistair, time to go home. Home, you awesome dog,' Fatty says, nudging Nameless Dog gently with his foot.

Nameless Dog stays put but opens both eyes and looks at me.

'Alistair,' I say. Hearing me call him by his new name, he gets up, licks Fatty's knee and follows me home.

Back at Chez Matchbox I find Fluffy, Mrs Ho and Ishmael smiling weakly at each other over strong cups of tea.

'You came back? You're not gone?' I say and give the gods a high five.

'I just went out to get some milk,' Mrs Ho says, giving me a puzzled look.

I tell the gods, okay, you got one over on me, I hope it makes you happy.

'I think we can manage with one car in the family for a while. Selling mine will get us the extra money we need to continue building,' Mrs Ho says. Her voice is a little crackly, but her hand is in Fluffy's and there is a steadfast glint in her eye.

'And between this guy I know, who's an expert bricklayer and plumber, and July and me we'll get the building done in the evenings after we come home from work and on the weekends,' Ishmael says. 'That will save a bit on labour.'

The steadfast look in Mrs Ho's eyes gets a bit blurry.

'My people built the pyramids, Julia. Building blood courses through my veins,' Ishmael says. 'It will be a piece of cake,' he adds desperately.

'I know you won't let me down, Ishmael,' Mrs Ho says, averting her eyes from his smooth hands that are clasped around his fat tummy. 'And July is going to speak to Miss Frankel about putting the dog in a kennel until she moves into a new house.'

I give a sort of a yelp.

'It's either the dog or me,' Mrs Ho says calmly.

I tell the gods that they really had fun with me today. That card of theirs was hidden way up the sleeves of their baggy togas.

I get up from the kitchen table and throw Sam Ho off the couch (in a cordial, friendly manner) and go and lie down with Alistair. After a while Fluffy comes over. 'You know we can't keep him,' he says gently. 'I'm sorry, April, but that was never going to happen.'

I swallow that golf ball which has by now completely rearranged my tonsils.

'How about a bird, or maybe a fish?' Fluffy says. 'It's your birthday in a couple of weeks. How about it, April?'

I tell Fluffy I don't want a pet for my birthday. In fact, I don't want to celebrate my birthday at all.

Soccer World Cup Update –
Days to Kick-off: 50

Match of the Day –
April-May and Fatty *vs* Dr Gainsborough

Ten

Group Shrinkage

I am making significant progress in my therapy sessions.

Dr Gainsborough and me have progressed from the running-away dream, to the falling-off-a-high-building dream and we are now obsessing over the failing-the-Maths-test dream.

It is Thursday morning, the second lesson after break (my second crazy class for the week), and Dr Gainsborough is lying on the floor in the Nutbox with his eyes closed. He raises his head from the carpet and I pause in my note-taking to make eye contact.

'But what do you think it means, April-May?'

I maintain eye contact – which inspires trust – and tell Dr Gainsborough that his dream of failing a Maths test indicates that he is afraid of forming close bonds with other members of the Homo sapiens species.

'Really? Do you think that could be it?'

I tell him that he either has intimacy issues or he's

scared of being trapped in a fridge or losing his teeth. Freud and me are in three minds about Dr Gainsborough's mental malady. The failing-a-Maths-test dream is a challenging one for a bursary kid like me to interpret because failing tests is not something I'm very good at.

Dr Gainsborough slumps back onto the floor and sighs. He says that this might explain why the closest relationships he's had in fifty-seven years have been with animals. And he pats Emily, who is dreaming (blindly) next to him on the carpet.

I look at my watch and tell Dr Gainsborough that our session is nearly over, but that next week we will explore the nature of his relationships with Emily and Emily's predecessors – there may be a pattern that will deliver critical insights. 'And healing,' I add, softly.

Dr Gainsborough's eyes glow behind his thick lenses. 'The dog I had before Emily had three legs. Her name was Tripod.' He is flushed with tender memories and sinks back onto the floor. 'The one before Tripod was deaf – from birth. And a cat I had around the same time couldn't purr.'

I tell Dr Gainsborough that we can explore this emerging pattern (that he only has relationships with damaged and sensorily challenged pets) next week. I say this in an even softer voice. A voice filled with empathy.

Dr Gainsborough gets up from the floor and says,

'Actually, April-May, we have another session in five minutes. You have a double today.'

I tell Dr Gainsborough that then in that case he can lie down again and we can continue exploring his deepest terrors. But he gives me a sort of gentle-but-firm smile and says, 'It's your turn, April-May. It's time you explored some healing.' Then he says that we're going to try something different. It's called group therapy.

I've done my research so Dr Gainsborough doesn't need to tell me that group therapy is exactly what the two words suggest – it's when two or more patients get psychoanalysed at the same time (in a group). It's not classic Freud – it was developed by some Americans in the early twentieth century (probably to save money).

I tell Dr Gainsborough that we already did group therapy with Mom when I first started his sessions. And neither of us was very chatty. In fact, I maintained operational silence throughout and Mom cried (throughout).

Dr Gainsborough replies that Mom wasn't a patient. He had invited her to my sessions to try and get a few things straightened out (something that didn't work – unfortunately). And that group therapy involves two or more actual patients (crazy people).

I settle down to enjoy the next hour with the girl from Grade Ten who is scared of swallowing her tongue – or maybe the Grade Eleven boy who can't stop himself from eating his hair. They both present an exciting opportunity for me to exercise my growing knowledge of psychoanalysis.

There is a knock at the office door, a pause and then Fatty walks (lumbers) in. I give Dr Gainsborough a slitty-eyed look. Then Fatty sees me and gives Dr Gainsborough a slitty-eyed look. But Dr Gainsborough does not meet our slitty eyes – he is too busy giving a grubby stain on the carpet a slitty-eyed look.

I stand up, give Fatty a nod and say, 'Have you ever tried group therapy before?' I use my cordial voice, the one I have developed to deal with him and Mom and Sarel The Leech and Sam Ho the boy-troll – in line with my pact with the gods.

'No,' Fatty says, in his version of the cordial voice, which he has cultivated since our last meeting in the park. 'Why?'

So Dr Gainsborough tells Fatty (and me for a second time) that we are about to embark on the non-Freudian form of healing called group therapy. And as he does so he rolls his eyes in apology at the little busts of Dr Sigmund Freud on his shelves. 'I am of the view that you and Ericca have much in common,' Dr Gainsborough says. 'I feel it in my gut.' And he pats his tummy.

I tell Dr Gainsborough that psychoanalysis is not a craft that one can practise based on what one has for breakfast. As someone who has single-handedly trained myself in the art of fact and logic I can tell him categorically that the only two things that Fatty and me have in common is that we are both bursary kids and we are both born of a woman.

Dr Gainsborough says that he had oats and a slice of pawpaw for breakfast and he is of the view that the two of us could help each other. 'Freud willing.' He manoeuvres me out of the way and takes the chair that I usually occupy during our sessions. Then he points Fatty and me to the two less comfortable chairs. 'And your last comment about you both being born of a woman shows much insight. You are an extremely perceptive young lady.'

Dr Gainsborough strokes his beard, arranges his features into a Freudian grimace and gives me a penetrating stare. Then he makes a note on his shrink pad. I have learned to read his scrawl from a two-metre distance and decipher the scribble as *Remember to pick up dog food on the way home.*

The rules about confidentiality for group therapy are even stricter than those for one-on-one confabs, so when I get home at the end of the day I can't write to tell Melly about my one-hour torture session with Fatty and Dr Gainsborough. Instead I tell Alistair, who has got until the end of next weekend at Chez Matchbox (before he gets boarded at Miss Frankel's house). Fluffy tells me that Miss Frankel tells him that there is no room at any of the thirteen kennels in Jozi, so Alistair has to board at the old house (with the caretaker). I tell Fluffy that I think Miss Frankel is trying to save on kennel fees – like she tried to save on a pool net (and look how badly that ended). But Fluffy says that Miss Frankel says that the caretaker will be glad of the company and will take care of Alistair along with the house.

In between him mauling Mrs Ho's toothbrush and digging a hole in the left side of the sofa, I tell Alistair that Dr Gainsborough started the session off with a little ditty which he wrote himself. It encompasses the principles and rationale of group therapy and he asked that Fatty and me hold hands with him while he recited it. It goes like this:

We are here to affirm, to nurture, to share and bear
Each other's burdens and show we care.
We have in common the issues that can break us,
And the wisdom that for sure will remake and heal
us.

Dr Gainsborough gave Fatty and me a copy of his composition, which is why I am aware of the line breaks. He said it was for us to look at if we are ever in doubt about group therapy. Like now, for instance.

I take out Dr Gainsborough's verse and read it out to

Alistair. He gives a sort of sniggery bark, which doesn't sound like the kind of response Dr Gainsborough was aiming for. 'Listen up,' I say. 'There's more.'

After the ditty-reading Dr Gainsborough asked Fatty and me to describe our mothers in one sentence. And this is when it started to get really interesting. I asked Dr Gainsborough if I could go first and Fatty said, 'You go, girl.' In his cordial voice.

This is the one sentence I used to describe my mother while Dr Gainsborough added to the shopping list on his shrink pad: 'My mother is five foot six, approximately sixty kilograms in weight and gaining and she has bushy hair and brown eyes and a darkish skin.'

Dr Gainsborough remarked (while making firm eye contact) that the twenty-six words I used to describe my mother could be used to describe about eighty per cent of the adult population on the African continent.

I replied that apart from the fact that I'd used twenty-five words, his observation was astute (and he mustn't forget to buy oven cleaner).

Then it was Fatty's turn.

When I mention Fatty's name Alistair spits out Mrs Ho's toothbrush and pricks up his ears.

Fatty's eyes flickered over Dr Gainsborough and me and then he said, 'I have never met my mother, but this is how I imagine her. My mother is five foot six, approximately sixty kilograms in weight and gaining and she has bushy hair and brown eyes and a darkish skin.'

Alistair gives a tiny jerk. Yes, just like Dr Gainsborough Alistair notices that Fatty used precisely the same words that I'd used to describe Mom. Freaky.

In the group therapy session Dr Gainsborough had rubbed his goatee like some dead Austrian psychoanalyst. 'Interesting,' he said. 'Fascinating.' And then, after what seemed like a three-hour pause, he turned to Fatty and said, 'It appears to me that you believe your birth mother has the same physical characteristics as April-May's mother. I wonder what it all means?'

Fatty surveyed Dr Gainsborough's expectant stare. Then his face lit up and he said slowly, in his gentle, cracked voice, 'Do you think, Dr Gainsborough, Sir, that April-May and me could have the same birth mother?'

Fatty's face was a montage of sweet innocence, wonder and earnest joy. But underneath that mask I detected pure wickedness.

The expression on Dr Gainsborough's face, however, was pure bliss. 'This is remarkable. A real breakthrough.' He beamed at us, his face radiating joy.

I looked at Fatty, and Fatty looked at me. And then Fatty looked at Dr Gainsborough's beatific face and turned away, shrugged, rolled his eyes and gave me a broad grin. And then he winked like a devil. And as I tell him this

Alistair rolls over onto his back, wags his tail and winks at me too.

It is in that winking moment in Dr Gainsborough's office that I recognise a kindred spirit. And Fatty and me become friends.

CROSSWORD CLUE 6 [seven down]:
Existing or happening now – or a thing
given to someone as a gift.

Eleven

The Birthday

The night before my birthday I dream.

I dream I am looking for something in Mom's drawers. I know I shouldn't be snooping in her private things but I'm trying to find something and I don't know what it is. My hand feels a book. It is a diary. I pick it up and start reading. But the words burn my hands and I drop the book and run.

I am running now and getting sucked up by concrete. I am failing my Maths test and I am falling, falling, falling. Then I wake up before I hit the ground and my ears echo with noise that sounds like 'Happy birthday! Happy birthday! Happy birthday!'

Mrs Ho, Fluffy and Sam Ho stand at my door and sing 'Happy birthday to you!' far too loudly for so early in the morning. Except I see that it's nearly midday and Fluffy says that it's about time I woke up because it's my special day and it would be a shame to waste it by sleeping it away.

And then they all make themselves comfortable on my bed, completely savaging my personal space bubble, and make me open my presents.

I get a thesaurus from Fluffy. 'Your very own,' he says. 'Now you won't have to borrow mine all the time.'

I tell Fluffy that I love my thesaurus. I adore it. I worship it.

He holds me tight for too long and says that he loves me more than anything else in the whole wide world and where was he looking when I got to be so big?

From Sam Ho I get a very complicated lock which requires a special code to get it to open. It's for my cupboards. 'If you use this I won't be able to get into your stuff and make you mad,' he says. The secretive look that I have seen on his face over the last few weeks is absent today. He has the look of the old Sam Ho, who I like sometimes when he is not being annoying.

I allow him to give me a quick hug and tell him that I love the lock. He says the code is easy to crack. He'll show me how.

Sam Ho also gives me a home-made birthday card, which he says that he's copied from an old Hallmark card. 'You can read it later,' he adds, the slyness returning to his face.

Mrs Ho hands me a paisley bag which she tells me contains 'girls' stuff' – two words that cause Sam Ho and

Fluffy to pull their mouths down and make funny faces at each other. I take a peek into the bag and see it's a fancy-schmancy razor and some special leg cream.

I tell Mrs Ho that I love it. ('I love it! I love it! I love it!') Now I won't have to deforest my legs with duct tape, which, take it from me, is as painful as having your lips chewed off your face by a flesh-eating virus. I give Mrs Ho a medium-length-but-sincere hug and let her hug me back.

There are also sixteen happy birthday text messages from Melly, consisting of fifteen kisses (one for every year) and a longer message saying that I am going to have to wait for my big-big present until she gets home.

Fluffy says we are going to spend the day celebrating my birthday. He says this very day fifteen years ago was the happiest day of his life. And then he starts reminiscing: 'You were born on a Tuesday, April. No wonder you are so full of grace.' Then he shakes his head. No, actually he is sure it was a Thursday – which means I have far to go . . .

I tell Fluffy that I was also born two months prematurely (on a Saturday), so I must have been a mighty small baby. 'How small was I? How much did I weigh when I was born?'

Fluffy says that as far as he can recall I was a healthy sized 3,6 kilograms, and then he starts grabbing at his hair.

Mrs Ho says that she's going to make tea, 'Anyone for a cup?' And then she tells Sam Ho to come along and help her with the labour-intensive task of putting teabags into the pot. She sort of runs for the kitchen, dragging Sam Ho behind her.

With Mrs Ho gone Fluffy says that he really, really can't recall how much I weighed at birth and I must ask Mom – who is banging on the front door, singing, 'Happy birthday to you, dear May-hay.' Sarel is standing behind her with his arms full of presents and his head covered in unevenly spaced plugs of hair. Grey, stringy, frizzy hair. The gods have heard me.

Sarel looks around nervously. 'Where's Killer?'

I tell Sarel that Killer is right behind him, about to rip the Achilles tendons from the backs of his ankles, and Sarel does an unendearing hop, skip and a jump into the house and onto the couch, where Alistair is watching reruns of *The Dog Whisperer*.

Alistair keeps his eyes glued to the television screen as guru Cesar barks (not whispers) at Daddy and Junior to repeat the exercise on how to demonstrate respect for the physical space of the alpha male. Then Alistair gives an impersonation of a life-threatening growl which Sarel interprets as 'get off my couch before I take a chunk of flesh out of your left ear'.

Mom and Sarel retreat into my bedroom and onto my bed – moving privacy issues to the top of my agenda in therapy – and make me open their presents.

There are Converse takkies and Adidas slip-slops and Diesel jeans and a docking station for my iPod – all of which Sarel says he paid for out of petty cash. He likes to make it known (loudly) that he's not a credit card man like Fluffy, who only has cash for the first five minutes on pay day before it gets swallowed up by debt.

After I open each present Mom says in a sort of begging voice, 'You do like it? It's the right size? It's your favourite colour? All the girls have them? Say you like it?' Things like that, which make me want to make her cry, so after every present I yawn and say, 'I suppose it's okay . . .' and 'It's fine if you like that sort of thing . . .'

There is one last present. 'Open it, May. Open it,' Mom says.

Her voice has a satisfactory quaver to it, so I say, 'Maybe later, opening so many presents is making me bored.'

Then Fluffy glances at Mom's crumpled face and says in a quiet voice, 'Open it, April.'

And I say, 'What the heck, let me get done with all these lame presents.'

The long and the short of it is that it is a computer. Not just any old computer. A ProBook 6540b. It does pretty much everything except fry eggs and massage your feet. I am grinning on the inside like a crazy fool. But on the outside I give an extra-long yawn.

Mom says that it's already fitted with a card that will

give me Internet access, which she will pay for every month. 'We can be Facebook buddies,' she says. 'And we can twitter each other all the time.'

'Tweet,' I say, correcting her.

'Tweet,' she says, 'Tweet, tweet, tweet, tweet, tweet, tweet, tweet.' She chants this merrily and gives a pleased if shaky smile, as though we have shared a moment.

Sarel says the computer isn't brand new. It's his old one (three months old) that the firm auctioned off when the senior partners converted to iPads the month before. 'The firm is doing extremely well. Yes, it is,' he says loudly, in case anyone is listening. Then he adds that the computer has all the apps and is set up for Skype video conferencing, so that I can share the best day of their lives with them. Then Sarel looks at Mom and says, 'Sorry, second-best day.'

I say, 'Best day? Second-best day?'

And Sarel says that the best day of his life was when he married Mom – exactly seven months and three hours ago. And that the second-best day of his life will be in two months, give or take a few hours – the birth of his son – my new baby brother. 'With this computer you can experience the birth of your brother in real time.' He sees the blank expression on my face. 'Precisely as it happens,' he says helpfully.

'My what?' I say. My voice sounds very loud and sort of high.

Sarel and Mom share a look and then he says. 'Ag, man, I'm sorry, Glorette, I know we agreed not to say . . .' And then his face breaks out into thirty-two different forms of stupid smile and he says, 'It's a boy. Can you believe it, May? It's a boy.'

I say I believe I need to get some air. And I grab the leash and Alistair, who is attached to the leash, and I run for the park.

While Alistair marks the swings and chews a hole in the tyre-seat I spy a couple of people under the plane trees. I'm not in the mood for company so I wander off in the opposite direction until Alistair pulls the leash out of my hands and sprints back the way we came.

'Hey, Alistair, you awesome-ist dog,' Fatty says as Alistair dives into his lunch box. 'Come here, boy.' Fatty puts his guitar aside, picks Alistair up and lets him give his face a wash. Then he allows him to have his way with his sandwiches.

I don't give Fatty's face a wash, but I say, 'Hey,' in a voice which has sort of grown into a natural friendly one of its own accord.

The past couple of group therapy sessions have encouraged within me a deep respect and admiration for Fatty. Between us, and our series of miraculous and earth-shattering breakthroughs around our mom issues, we are driving Dr Gainsborough completely cuckoo. And it is this shared mission which has laid the building blocks for my friendship with Fatty.

'Hey, Ricky, my buddy, don't stop singing,' a voice which make my toes curl up with joy says.

Sebastian calls Fatty 'Ricky', a short version of Ericca – which is a whole lot cooler than calling him Fatty (which is a long, cruel version of Fat).

Sebastian raises his head from his guitar and his eyes gleam when he sees me.

'Hey, Bella.'

I say, 'Hey, Bas,' a little listlessly, and he says, 'In a funk?'

I say, 'You can say that again.'

And he says, 'In a funk?'

And I say, 'It's my birthday.' And both Sebastian and Fatty nod, as though they get precisely what I am talking about.

Fatty says he doesn't even know when his birthday is, except it's sometime in December. 'I was abandoned in the locker room of a soccer club when I was a baby. The only thing my parents gave me was my name, which they wrote on a piece of paper and tied to my foot.'

And what a name it is, I think, but I don't say it, for obvious reasons which have something to do with the name I was given by my own forward-thinking parents.

Sebastian says, 'That's nothing, try this.' It turns out that on his birthday his parents give him a credit

112

card and drop him off at the mall. He has to buy his own presents.

Fatty and me laugh and say things like 'that's really tough' and stuff like that, so Sebastian adds that sometimes his parents get the day of his birthday wrong and he has to do it a day early. And we laugh even louder.

Then they both look to me for my sob story, but I just shrug. I don't tell them that I found my mom's old diaries. And read them. I don't tell them what I discovered about my birthday because when I even think it, let alone try and say it, it feels like someone's playing pinball in my head. Instead I say I have to go home and eat some birthday cake. And I do.

And then I have my birthday bath. A bath all of my own, with litres and litres of boiling-hot water which I don't have to share with the other residents of Chez Matchbox in the interests of beating the electricity bill.

Then, before I go to bed on my birthday night, I open Sam Ho's birthday card. There is a drawing of Fluffy and Sam Ho and Mrs Ho and me. Inside Sam Ho has written in his perfect handwriting: *Mazel tov on the day of your bar mitzvah, with lots of love from your aunty and uncle Sam Ho*. There are three possible explanations for this birthday message. The first is that Sam Ho is crazy. The second is that he has a kinky sense of humour. And then there is a third explanation.

113

I think about Sam Ho lying to Fluffy about not getting my note in the first week back at school. I think about him nearly killing himself by taking the wrong tablets for his allergies. I think about it some more and then I get up from my bed and go through to the lounge.

Alistair The Protector is fast asleep on the couch and doesn't stir. And on the floor next to him is Sam Ho. 'I know your terrible secret, Sam Ho,' I whisper. But he is sleeping, so he doesn't hear me.

Soccer World Cup Update –
Days to Kick-off: 40

Match of the Day –
Alistair The Awesome-ist *vs* The World

Twelve

Rhonda's Secret

Sundays are Building Days. That's when Fluffy and Ishmael and this guy who Ishmael knows (the whizz bricklayer and plumber) build the en suite bathroom for the soccer-mad billionaire from Europe who is going to be spending four weeks at Chez Matchbox during the Soccer World Cup.

Except that, for the guy who Ishmael knows, Sunday is also the day he plays cricket with his brother and fixes his mother-in-law's washing machine and has barbecues with his family before watching the rugby.

So, Fluffy and me never meet the expert bricklayer and plumber. And Ishmael and Fluffy have to get on with transforming the garage into a luxury suite on their own while Mrs Ho bites her lips into one shrivelled line and stays out of the way in case she says something she'll regret later.

This particular Sunday, the day after my birthday, is also

the day that Alistair gets to go to Miss Frankel's abandoned house with the killer swimming pool to live with the caretaker until his new accommodation is secured. It was either Alistair or Mrs Ho. So Alistair got to go.

Alistair and me had spent the previous week trying to change his destiny by attuning our thoughts to the 'staying vibrations' in the universe the way Rhonda Byrne in her best-selling book *The Secret* describes it.

Rhonda's big secret is that focused positive thinking can have life-changing results. But as hard as we tried we didn't manage to achieve harmony with this particular outcome and so Alistair is finally leaving.

I've packed a special bag for Alistair, containing his leash, Sarel's wig, a photo from a TV mag of Cesar, Daddy and Junior and a snack pack filled with tasty dog treats (Mrs Ho's loofah, Fluffy's hairbrush and a couple of shoes that lost their partners in a previous snack frenzy).

It's as though Alistair knew the end of the road was coming for him at Chez Matchbox. He spent the previous three days sampling every corner of the house and watching back-to-back reruns of *The Dog Whisperer*. He also had trouble sleeping and would crawl into my bed in the early hours of the morning and only drop off after I'd read him a couple of chapters of *The Secret* and told him positively, definitely and categorically that his destiny was to stay with me at Chez Matchbox.

I keep the faith until the hour of departure arrives and then I have to admit that I have failed Rhonda and Alistair by not being focused and positive enough. I tell Alistair so sorry and that I'll come visit whenever I can, and that I'll bring Fatty with me. At the sound of that name Alistair unlocks his jaw from the side of the front door and allows Fluffy and me to drag him into the stiff-mobile.

We leave Ishmael mixing concrete. One part cement, two parts sand and three parts gravel. 'Don't make it too runny – it must be like cake mixture,' I shout. I checked this out for him on Google using Heaven – my old/new birthday computer.

There are four words to describe my attachment to Heaven and the magical Interweb world that it allows me to enter: I am completely addicted. I feel the same way a three-month-old baby must feel when she tastes sugar for the first time. I am off my head.

Miss Frankel's house is in a suburb with lots of trees and almost as many security guards. There are no signs of children playing in the street. In fact, the ratio of trees and security guards to children playing in the streets is 3:2:0.

I tell Alistair that he is going to lead a peaceful life – no irritating kids wanting to play with him all the time and dragging him off to the park for walks – with plenty of oxygen and security on tap. Alistair ignores me and tries to dig a tunnel under Fluffy's seat.

118

Fluffy parks the stiff-mobile outside the house and presses the intercom button which says *Caretaker*. We wait five minutes until the caretaker answers. He says he was outside taking care of the garden and that his name is Kindness.

Kindness takes a critical look at the spattered stiff-mobile and then takes an even more critical look at Alistair. Reaching down he picks him up (uncarefully and unkindly) by his front legs. Like he is some ballroom dancer. Except he's not. He's a dog. And so Alistair gives a yelp and tries to amputate Kindness's hand from his wrist.

Then Kindness gives Alistair a playful smack across the snout and Alistair yelps again, because it was quite a hard playful smack. I say, 'Let me.' And I put the leash on Alistair and follow Kindness onto the premises and to his cottage, which has a courtyard where Alistair will be living until Miss Frankel sells the house and moves into her new abode. The courtyard is half the size of my bedroom at Chez Matchbox and is filled with nothing – nothing, that is, except lots of hard concrete. Over the courtyard wall is the garden with the killer swimming pool. I am glad that Alistair is not tall enough to look over the wall to see the expanse of chlorinated water that claimed his mom and nineteen brothers and sisters in the mass drowning four months ago.

Fluffy says, 'We really, really must be going, April.'

'Not until I know where Alistair will be sleeping,' I say.

Kindness says that he'll sleep with him in his cottage. But that doesn't fool me. 'Where is his water bowl?' I ask. 'And his plate of Epol crackers?'

Kindness says that it's inside the cottage and that he needs to get on with taking care of Miss Frankel's house now, so goodbye.

I put Alistair's things in the corner of the courtyard and Fluffy and me leave. I don't look back because if I do I'm afraid I may do something uncharacteristic, like leaking bodily fluids from my facial orifices.

As we get into the stiff-mobile I hear a mournful howl coming from the back of Miss Frankel's house. And then it stops mid-howl, as though someone or something walloped it across the snout. Fluffy and me don't talk on the way home.

When we arrive back at Chez Matchbox I find Fatty mixing concrete while Ishmael spurs him on with encouraging words like, 'put your back into it', 'faster-faster' and 'not so much water, it must be like cake mix'.

I tell Ishmael, 'It's your turn now, you lazy bones!' and take Fatty on a guided tour of Chez Matchbox. I introduce him to Sam Ho, who nearly swallows his eyeballs and says something like, 'I heard you were big, but you're bigger.' And Fatty says something like, 'And I'm still growing, so watch this space.' And then he stretches up and blows air into his cheeks so that he looks even bigger and scarier than before.

I catch Sam Ho's eye before it pops out of his head and give him a look which says, 'I know your terrible secret and you need to fess up.' But before Sam Ho looks away he gives me a look that says, 'You can't make me, and if you rat me out you'll die from facial boils and dandruff.' It's a stand-off between Sam Ho and me.

The tour of Chez Matchbox is quick – the sour-sour tree out back where Alistair spent his awesome days and the couch in front of the television where Alistair spent his awesome nights. Fatty and me spend a few minutes in respectful silence in front of Alistair's couch and then Fatty says he bets Alistair is going to be happy in that big garden with Kindness The Caretaker, and I think of the small concrete courtyard and the caretaker's unkind face, but I don't say I bet he won't.

Fatty is visiting me at Chez Matchbox to admire Heaven. And to educate me on the finer points of social networking. He is going to help me set up a Facebook account, so that I can network with my wide circle of friends (Melly, Sebastian and him). And he is also going to walk me through Twitter and set up an email account, so I can write long letters to Melly which she will be able to access on The Goddess and not have to wait for snail mail or read my gimpy text messages.

Fifteen minutes later I am a member of a community of five hundred million Facebook friends. Fatty is my first Facebook friend and I have sent friend requests to Sebastian and Melly and Rhonda Byrne and Mark Zuckerberg, who is the brainbox behind the Facebook concept (and so is obviously a very sociable kind of a guy).

I also have a Gmail account – hotcalendargirl@gmail.com – and a Twitter account – @hotcalendargirl. This concept is Fatty's big idea. He says I must claim my identity and make the brand work for me. Running away from one's name will only cause one to be miserable.

I say, 'Sure thing, Ricky.' Which is what he has asked me to call him now that we have achieved friend status.

Fatty says a person can leverage the Interweb to do just about anything (except scrub your back or dice a tomato), but sometimes it doesn't have the answers to the questions you most want to know.

'Just google it. Google has the answers to everything,' I tell Fatty.

But he says, 'No, Calendar Girl, Google can't tell me what I most want to know.'

I look at Fatty and I see the small picture of my face in his left eye. And I know that he can see his face in mine. And I don't blink. And neither does he. And I tell him that he can tell me what he most wants to know. And he says that he knows he can.

He says what he most wants to know is when we're eating lunch because he's starving. And I tell him that he doesn't have to joke around any more. I'm his Facebook friend; he can trust me. I say, 'Tell me, Ricky.' So he does.

'I want to know who my parents are. My real parents. Or at least my mom. I want to find her and ask her why she dumped me. Why she didn't think I was worth hanging on to. I'm so sick of feeling worthless and angry.' His cracked voice cracks so hard I'm scared it's going to splinter into tiny pieces.

My face starts swimming around in Fatty's left eye and I feel my eyes starting to act up too, so I blink. And so does he. And then I say, 'I'm also starving. Let's eat.'

We are working our way through several loaves of bread and a month's supply of school-lunch tuna when Fluffy screams into the kitchen, grabbing at his hair. It's an emergency. He needs Heaven. He has forgotten the quantities for concrete. Their concrete is too runny. It's not like cake mixture. The bricks are slipping and sliding and not becoming a wall.

I could tell Fluffy the answer – one part cement, two parts sand and three parts gravel and go easy on the water – but I don't. Because I think, like Rhonda Byrne, that some secrets need to be shared – and I don't want to die of boils and dandruff. So instead I tell Fluffy that I'll get

Heaven. And that I'll google concrete-mixing. And because I'm elbow-deep in tuna-mayo sandwiches and Fluffy and Ishmael are dripping in concrete mix Sam Ho can read out the recipe. And then I yell for Sam Ho and tell him that Fluffy needs him this instant. And I give him Heaven and then I watch.

Sam Ho sits on the stairs outside the kitchen and Ishmael and Fluffy look to him and Aunty Google for wisdom. Sam Ho stares at the screen and Ishmael says, 'We haven't got all day, china, we've got a wall to build.'

And then Mrs Ho comes into the kitchen and stands behind Sam Ho. But she doesn't say anything because she doesn't want to get involved. And she doesn't want to discourage the workforce. So she stays quiet. And bites her cadaverous lips.

Finally Sam Ho says, 'Three hundred and fifty grams of sand and two hundred and twenty millilitres of gravel and two hundred grams of cement.'

Fluffy says, 'Stop horsing around, Sam Ho, and give us the real deal. This wall won't build itself.' But Sam Ho just repeats what he said.

And then Mrs Ho unzips her tight lips and says, 'Sam Ho, this isn't funny. They are trying to build a wall.'

Sam Ho's face collapses in the middle and he says, 'I'm not messing around, this is what the recipe for concrete says.'

Mrs Ho peers down at Heaven. 'Why on earth are you reading out the recipe for carrot cake?' she asks.

Sam Ho looks at me. His face is pale and there are bruises under his eyes. I look at him back and I say in my gentle voice – the one I use when he's taken the skin off his knees or dropped his Coco Pops in his lap – 'It's okay, Sam Ho, you can let go now.'

And I take Heaven from him and I say to Mrs Ho, 'Sam Ho has something he needs to tell you.'

CROSSWORD CLUE 7 [seven across]:
A piece of work that involves collecting detailed
information about something or to make your voice
loud enough to be heard at a distance.

Thirteen

The Lawyer

Trinity College has given us a long weekend. Yeeha!

There are three good things about these five days of leisure. The first good thing is that my best friend Melly is coming home. Finally.

After two major operations at Groote Schuur Hospital and a month of post-operative care at her Uncle James' guest house in Franschhoek, she has been certified well and truly better.

The second good thing is that Fatty (Ricky), Sebastian (Bas) and me (April-May) have been given permission by Miss Frankel (Geraldine) to take Alistair (The Awesome-ist) out for the day (Sunday).

Fluffy is going to take me in the stiff-mobile to collect Alistair from Miss Frankel's house (which is still for sale) and will drop us off at the park, where we will be met by Fatty and Sebastian, bearing bones for Alistair and a picnic for me.

The third good thing about the long weekend is that Fluffy and Ishmael are putting the final finishing touches to Chez Matchbox's luxury bedroom with en suite bathroom. It's either this or Mrs Ho is going to commit abusive acts which infringe upon their rights to life and dignity. She says this through her teeth because her lips have gotten so thin they have disappeared.

Fluffy says, 'It's a piece of cake. No worries, Julia, things will be shipshape by the end of the long weekend.' They only have the plumbing and electricity to do. And then they must tidy up a couple of minor things, like the dozen or so too many air vents in the one wall where the bricks don't fit properly and the crop of unseemly cracks in the other wall (runny concrete effect). And then there's the small matter of a few coats of paint. That should do it.

Mrs Ho says that she doesn't want to know any more about it, she has her hands full with Sam Ho, who will be spending most of the five-day holiday doing a battery of tests to try and discover why on earth he is unable to read. This was Sam Ho's big secret. He can't read for toffee and had been busking it all along – until I bust him in my underhand and treacherous way. Sam Ho says that he'll never speak to me again for blowing his secret (a bit of a bonus, especially in the mornings, when I am not at my most conversational), but really I think he is relieved that he doesn't have to live a double life any more.

Mrs Ho is still trying to get to the bottom of Sam Ho's inability to decipher the written word. Does Sam Ho have a problem with his eyes? Or his ears? Or did he suffer an undetected brain trauma when he was involved in the tragic accident that removed Mr Ho from Planet Earth nearly two years ago? Or is Sam Ho just a dumb chop (my suggestion and not one of Mrs Ho's favourites).

Mrs Ho is in a big funk because she thinks that she's the dumb chop for being the deputy principal at Trinity College and never noticing that her own son can barely read his name, let alone tell the difference between a recipe for carrot cake and one for concrete. I've never been a slave to winning popularity contests so until she has it figured out I'm going big with the 'dumb chop' diagnosis.

Apart from all the good stuff that is happening this weekend, there is the one bad thing – I have to spend the first two days of the holiday with Mom and Sarel at their home in Pretoria.

Fluffy says that it's only fair. During the past two months I have barely spent a weekend with Mom owing to a rash of debilitating illnesses which I have mysteriously attracted since the onset of my addiction to *House*.

For all those without DStv, *House* is a medical series about a super-smart doctor with an attractive limp called Gregory House. He walks a bit like Sebastian, except

Sebastian doesn't have an über-cool cane (or a dangerous addiction to Vicodin).

With the assistance of Dr House I have had the symptoms for intracranial berry aneurysm (severe headaches), Fabry disease (ringing in the ears and vertigo) and, Dr House's favourite, lupus – fatigue, aches and an unexplained fever (brought on by hot facecloths).

Mom keeps telling Fluffy, 'May's bluffing . . .', and Fluffy keeps asking, 'April, are you bluffing?', and I keep saying it just the way Dr House says it, 'Everybody lies.' And Fluffy keeps winking and telling Mom that I'm really, really not feeling well, so maybe next weekend.

In any case, in the three weeks since my birthday Fluffy has had to tile the shower, screed the floor and plaster the walls, and none of this could have been done without Heaven, Aunty Google, YouTube and me.

I don't know what we did before I got Heaven. You want to know how to debone a chicken? Aunty Google tells me – and the masterclass chef on YouTube shows me how. You want to know how to give yourself a tattoo, perform a tracheotomy with a Bic pen, give a French manicure, keep a bee farm, assassinate a minor world leader, crochet a hot-water bottle cover? The answer to any of these and how to do a million other things come courtesy of YouTube and Aunty Google in Heaven.

Fluffy drops me off at Mom and Sarel's house in the

posh suburb of Waterkloof in the stiff-mobile. 'Just give your mom a break, April,' he says. 'She loves you more than anything else in the whole wide world.'

I tell him to make sure that he shakes the paint tin properly before opening it, otherwise the colour on the walls of the en suite will be uneven.

Mom greets me with a troublesome hug and says she hopes I like the way she has redecorated my bedroom – soon to be my new baby brother's bedroom.

I tell her I have no time for interior décor. I have a school project to do and I need peace and quiet. And I need to do my project in Sarel's office.

'Think again, May,' Mom says. 'Not a chance. That's Sarel's business office.' It's out of bounds, even to her.

I say I need to work in a space that has been inhabited by a great man who has given birth to deep thoughts that have led to brilliant acts. I need to work in Sarel's office. 'I want to be inspired and infused with the man's wisdom and intellect. I need to share his space.'

Mom says, 'Goodness me then, of course, you must do your project in Sarel's office.' And then she smiles like she's just guzzled down a six pack of Vicodin.

I chuck my stuff down and set up camp on Sarel's desk, throwing myself body and soul into *The Lawyer* – my own reality show. I correspond with the number one chief at the Lost Souls Orphanage in Soweto, the big cheese at the Johannesburg Department of Welfare, the head honcho at the Department of Home Affairs (Braamfontein) and several other bigwigs at various other institutions.

I want answers. I am a hotshot lawyer from an ace legal firm in Pretoria and I have his stationery and signature and fax machine to prove it. I demand answers in the jargon of a legal eagle, jargon that is neatly set out in hundreds of legal documents that reside in Heaven (documents that Sarel The Sucker forget to erase from his computer before bequeathing it to me for my birthday).

I instruct the institutions that unless they play ball, and provide me with the full disclosure necessary to unlock the mystery of Project Fatty, I am going to make them wish that they were eating a plate of goat's tonsils or having their body parts dissected by a swarm of sand fleas (depending if they want to play *Fear Factor* or *Survivor* instead of playing *The Lawyer* with me).

The answers I want pertain to the circumstances of Fatty's birth. He wants to know who his parents are. And between Sarel's legal firm and me we are going to help him find them. Or, at least, find his mom. I instruct all the big cheeses to email their responses to my private secretary: April-May February at hotcalendargirl@gmail.com.

I spend the rest of my stay with Mom and Sarel ensconced in Sarel's office playing FarmVille and making friends with fabulous and interesting people all over the world. My three thousand and six Facebook friends include a set of identical Eskimo twins from Greenland, an exotic dancer at a three-star hotel in Cairo and a member of the Danish royal family.

And when I'm not Interwebbing I'm ignoring discussions between Mom and Sarel about the second happiest day of their lives, which is just around the corner.

Mom is now certifiably with child. There is no mistaking the soccer ball below her waist for a bit of pigging out (oops, sorry, Fatty) over Christmas, or one too many chocolate marshmallow eggs on Easter Sunday. The only thing that needs to be discussed is the How of the Having.

Mom wants a home birth. Sarel wants Mom hooked up to every available piece of birthing equipment ever invented. As a compromise they are going for a home-birth-from-home delivery, which is a fantastic piece of marketing pap which only an expert spin doctor like Mom could fall for. She gets to have her baby with the aid of a midwife and a world-class gynae in a first-world hospital room which has been decorated like the entrance hall of a medium-sized house (where apparently most home-birthers have their babies).

Between the birthing option discussions, the packing and repacking of the home-birth-from-home suitcase, the shuffling about of the furniture in Baby's room and the birthing exercises that I am required to time using an Olympic stopwatch, the two days with Mom and Sarel are the stuff of nightmares. I am packed and ready to flee when Fluffy picks me up on Sunday morning.

At the exact moment the doorbell rings Mom and Sarel are in the midst of yet another name debate. The favourites are Sarette and Glorel, which are the expectant couple's combo compromises. And then there is Elvis-Jacobus, after Sarel's father, which is limping behind in blue suede shoes – but is still a close third. Even I feel a pinch of pity for the poor kid. Whichever way it goes he's screwed.

Fluffy parks the stiff-mobile outside Miss Frankel's soon-to-be-hopefully-sold house in the leafy street and I buzz kindly for the caretaker. Kindness appears ten minutes later, pulling Alistair behind him.

I call, 'Alistair!', but he doesn't respond. Instead he keeps his tail fixed firmly between his legs just in case it springs loose and gives me a heck-it's-nice-to-see-you-April-May wag. I say 'Alistair!' again and he growls.

Fluffy gets busy with the old bath towel on the back seat – to minimise the hair in the stiff-mobile – while I tell Kindness that we will have Alistair back by five o'clock.

Kindness hands me the leash and I coax Alistair onto the seat. He climbs in growling like I'm sticking needles into the backs of his knees, or his eardrums, or something.

We drive off and Fluffy says, 'Crap!' and 'Ruddy!' and 'Stuffing heck!' and 'Bloody!', which are the words Fluffy deploys when he is emotionally challenged about an issue. But he tends to use one of these child-unfriendly words at a time – not a whole string of them.

'What are you going on about?' I ask as Fluffy stops the car a few metres down the road from Miss Frankel's house and reaches over to the back seat, where Alistair is crouching.

Fluffy says, 'Just hang on a second with that growling, boy . . .' and parts the fur around Alistair's neck to reveal scabs. Alistair bares his teeth, but Fluffy is undeterred. He nudges Alistair onto his back and the tummy is displayed, scratched red and raw.

I think of Dr House and Chase and Foreman and Thirteen in that room of theirs, writing symptoms on the whiteboard. *A canine patient with an altered disposition, displaying antisocial tendencies, with neck scabs and tummy scratched raw.* I don't need Dr House or a calculator to add it all up and come up with the answer.

Alistair The Awesome-ist has been tortured.

Soccer World Cup Update –
Days to Kick-off: 19

Match of the Day –
Melly, Fatty and Me *vs* Destiny

Fourteen

Dissing Destiny

Everything you do and everything that happens to you has already been determined by forces over which you have no control.

Weirding you out? Well, try this: The script for your life has already been written. From the moment you are born it is simply up to you to mouth the words and perform the actions on life's stage.

If you are one of the people who think this way, it goes without saying that Emily, Dr Gainsborough's golden retriever, was destined to be blind. It was Emily's mother's destiny to sit on Emily's head when she was three hours old (and not on one of her other, more agile puppy siblings), thus sentencing her to a life of darkness.

People who believe in the fixed course of destiny would concur that it is my fate to eat Weet-Bix sans milk for breakfast this morning – as it was Sam Ho's destiny to hog (oops, sorry, Fatty) the milk by having a big mug of hot chocolate last night. And that it is Fluffy's destiny to get his ear chewed off by Mrs Ho for not stocking up on box milk for these droughts and thereby causing her to drink her morning tea black.

However, today it is my kismet to conclude that people who believe that everything has been mapped out and planned by the Big Architect In The Sky are plain wrong. They are Big Losers. And I will not be Facebook friends with these people – the ones who take a punch in the face from life with a 'Thank you so very much. I deserve this. Hit me again, I'm not going to duck'.

This is a summary of the speech I give in the park on Sunday morning after Fluffy drops Alistair and me off for our picnic. I stand on the swing, holding onto the ropes and call my troops to engage in total revolution against Alistair's fate. 'No, we cannot!' (allow this to happen) is my cry. 'Can we?' And, 'No, we cannot!' is the answer. Which is sort of a neat and tidy. I'm thinking of selling the speech to Mr Barack Obama, the President of the United States of America, when he runs for his second term.

Fatty and Sebastian punctuate my every utterance with cries of 'Right on!', 'Bring it on!' and 'Get it on!', while Alistair gets on with getting the past few weeks of pain and suffering out of his system by ripping out every winter bulb in the freshly planted bed by the plane trees. Then he marks my new winter shoes, which are perched at the foot of the swings, before lying down a couple of feet away from Fatty and whimpering.

Fatty is in a fair state over Alistair. He keeps saying things like 'I can't believe how thin he's got . . .' and 'I can't believe how grumpy he's got . . .' and 'Have you seen the pitiful state of his neck?' Stuff like that.

I can see he's really cut up about it all because he offers Alistair his wallet (emptied of cash) to chew on. When Alistair sniffs at the leather, and turns his head away and howls, Fatty says, 'We really, really have to do something.'

Sebastian says that in his view we have three options to consider in dealing with the SAC (Sad Alistair Conundrum). The light filters through the leaves and dapples his face golden as he speaks; his lime-green eyes hold mine. My heart beats a little faster and my eyes start misting over. I lean forward, eager to hear his words of wisdom.

Sebastian says the first option is that we can leave Alistair in the care of Kindness The Caretaker and allow him to be tortured 24/7 in his Guantánamo Bay Courtyard with the tacit approval of the deaf, dumb and brain-dead who inhabit the leafy Jozi suburb in which said courtyard is to be found.

Fatty and me say this is a rubbish option. Sebastian replies that it's lucky for us then that he has two others. The second option is that we kidnap Kindness The Caretaker and keep him in our own courtyard of torture and force-feed him on Boss and Butch (instead of Husky, which is every canine's choice of tinned food). That will teach him.

Fatty and me say, 'Interesting . . .'

And then there's the third option.

'You could report the caretaker to the SPCA.'

This suggestion comes from behind me and is made by a very small voice. I look over my shoulder and nearly fall off the swing as I recognise the face that comes with the voice.

It's Melly. A little taller, a little skinnier, slightly more freckled of face and longer in hair, but one hundred per cent my old dear Melly – home a day early to surprise me. Surprise!

Sebastian grumbles that this wasn't his third option while Melly and me throw ourselves at each other for a good five minutes.

When we are done Melly says a cool hello to Sebastian and gives him a look which says, 'You're trouble and I don't think being away at boarding school has changed you one bit.' And then I introduce Melly to Fatty.

Melly looks at Fatty and Fatty looks at Melly. I look at both of them looking at each other. I see a small, freckly girl breathing with determination and purpose through her nose and an over-large boy with a greasy stain down the front of his T-shirt.

My best friend and my second-best friend. I am holding thumbs that they will like each other just a tiny bit. But I needn't have worried. Within two minutes they are acting like they are best friends. Correction, second-best friends, because I'm Melly's best friend.

'He's got such presence, such stature . . . such . . .' Melly says about Fatty. She whispers it behind her hand as she gives me an absent-minded push on the swing; her freckles standing out like ellipses all over her flushed face.

'Is she real? She's so delicate. Will she break?' Fatty says to me a few minutes later. His voice has sunk to a broken croak and I can hardly hear him.

'What? What did you say about Melly?' I yell at him.

His face takes on a moist glow and he says, 'Shush! She'll hear you!' And then he goes and throws a couple of bulbs around for Alistair.

Melly then hisses a 'What are you doing hanging around with him again, haven't you learned your lesson?' at me, nodding at Sebastian.

I tell Melly that people change. Look at me. Last year I was a troublemaker bent on hell and destruction and this year I am a role model for the virtues of restraint and good sense.

'You didn't need to change. You were always who you are. And he is who he is – a slacker, and a no-good chancer,' Melly says. 'He's going to drag you down again.'

I tell Melly that Fatty hangs out with Sebastian too. They're in a band together (so there). Melly says, 'Oh . . .' And then she says that she hopes that he doesn't drag Fatty down as well.

It's time for the picnic and I spread the blanket and set out the food while Melly goes and throws sticks for Alistair and Fatty (who watches Melly throw sticks but doesn't run after them with Alistair) and Sebastian lounges on the grass watching me.

The stick-throwing is completely pointless. If you are a Big Loser with fatalist tendencies you know it is already written in the cosmos that Alistair will rip each stick to pieces, necessitating a new stick for each throw. And the ones that you throw too far will just be ignored.

These people who believe that everything that happens in your life has been determined before your parents were even a blink in their parents' eyes will say that we are all here, at this precise moment, because that is where we are supposed to be – even if it is doing something as useless as throwing sticks for Alistair.

I think differently. I don't think we are destined to be here, or there, or anywhere else. It can change. Because we can change it.

It is thus scripted that while having our picnic of lamb-stew-and-pickle sandwiches and drinking Oros, courtesy of Fatty's pale-faced mom, Sebastian, Melly, Fatty and me decide that we should act to change Alistair's circumstances and his home address.

It's a sensible plan. It's Melly's plan. She goes over it twenty times just so we are all 'on the same page'. She keeps on and on until I'm about ready to rip the page out of her hand and shove it into my ears.

This is the plan: each one of us will (independently) telephone the SPCA and report the brutal conditions under which Alistair is being held. And when Alistair is rescued by the canine-loving agents of the SPCA, Fatty will make moves to adopt Alistair as his own beloved pet. Foolproof.

Fatty checks with me again that I'm fine with this and I tell him, of course, he must have Alistair. Because I can't. And it's not like I won't see Alistair all the time, seeing as he and I have best-friend (except for Melly) status. And Fatty looks at Melly, and then he looks at me, and he says that that's exactly how he sees it too, of course.

Melly appears very satisfied with the outcome of our/ her plot. Sebastian, however, appears less satisfied. He keeps on trying to introduce his third option, but without Fatty's support he gives up and says, 'All right then, let's call the SPCA.'

After the picnic, Fatty's mother comes to fetch him and Alistair, to take them to their respective homes. This is the first time that Fatty's mother has met Alistair and she says, 'Goodness, this dog needs a bath.' She wrinkles her nose and I see Fatty bristling.

'He just looks dirty. He doesn't smell,' he snaps.

Her pale skin flushes and she says, 'I didn't mean . . .' And she puts out her hand to touch Fatty's arm. He flinches and she lets her hand fall to her side. There is an edgy silence and then she asks if anyone wants a lift home.

I say, 'I'm good.' I'm walking home with Melly. She's got a big-big birthday present waiting for me that I know she's dying for me to open. And then I look over at my best friend to share the kind of smile that best friends give each other.

Except that she seems not to have heard me and is smiling and nodding at Fatty. Yes, she'll go with him to return Alistair to Kindness The Caretaker. It's good that she sees the concrete courtyard and the killer swimming pool for herself, so she can report accurately and honestly to the officials at the SPCA. Then Melly leaps into the back of Fatty's mom's car with just a quick wave and a smile at her best friend (oh, that's me).

Fatty settles Alistair into the front seat and gets into the back seat with Melly. She fits perfectly under his armpit. She turns to look at him and he looks at her. Their profiles are like pieces of the same puzzle that are made to fit. His nose above hers and her chin below his.

Once they have driven off Sebastian and me hang out together. We spend a half-hour deploying the bulbs that Alistair hasn't pulped to play ducks and drakes. There isn't a lake to skim the bulbs on so we fling them like frisbees across the road. As close to the ground as possible. And when they manage to dodge oncoming car wheels Sebastian shouts, 'Awesome!'

And when they don't – and bounce up and hit oncoming car windscreens – I say, 'Maybe we should play something else?'

Sebastian says that he doesn't want to talk behind his best pal Ricky's back, but he thinks the SPCA Scheme for the SAC (Sad Alistair Conundrum) is totally lame.

I say that it's Melly's plan and I would never say a word against my best friend, but I think it's complete rubbish too.

Sebastian flops down next to me and starts plucking long blades of grass and threading them through my toes. My toes feel ticklish. My head feels ticklish. Sebastian makes me feel ticklish all over.

He stops for a minute with his toe tickling and says, 'Hey, Bella.'

I say, 'Hey, Bas.'

He says, 'Do you want to hear my third option. I think you'll like it.'

I say, 'Tell me, Bas.'

CROSSWORD CLUE 8 [eight down]:
Physically disturbed or set in motion.

Fifteen

The Vapours

The day before yesterday, at the crack of dawn, twenty men dressed in identical work gear moved onto our school sports fields and ripped up the turf. And as one set of trucks removed the old turf from the school premises, another set of trucks delivered enough pipe to lay a world-class irrigation system.

The next day (yesterday), at the crack of dawn, the same twenty men spent the day digging trenches, laying the pipes for the irrigation system and filling everything back in again.

On the third day (today), yet again the same twenty men rose at first light from their beds to come to our school with trucks filled with new turf, which they laid before walking up and down on it so it settled in nicely.

Tomorrow, one person will probably flick a switch to get the new fields watered with the new irrigation system while the twenty men in the identical work gear rip up some other school's sport fields or have a lie-in.

The three-day turf-relaying exercise has caused major excitement at Trinity College – and it isn't the way the twenty men toss the squares down the line and then plonk them into the ground, beating each one with a spade until moving onto the next. No, the hysteria is being caused by What Is Coming After.

The What is Italy's finest. Fabio Cannavaro, Daniele de Rossi, Gianluigi Buffon and the rest. They are Italy's team for the Soccer World Cup and they – the 2006 World Champions and the winners of three other world cups – have chosen Trinity College from several thousand schools in South Africa as their training venue ahead of their fifth World Cup victory.

It is not only the students at Trinity College who are in a state this week. There are several other people in my intimate circle who are also feeling far from mellow.

The first person is Fluffy. The reason for his frenzy is the perverse plumbing in the deluxe suite at Chez Matchbox. The second person is Mrs Ho, whose passive-aggressive, thin-lipped state is directly related to the water-fall that pours from the kitchen ceiling every time Fluffy turns on the shower in the new bathroom that is soon to be occupied by our cash-rich soccer tourist.

'I did everything exactly the way that man did it on

YouTube,' Fluffy says, ripping out his hair. 'What could have gone wrong, April-May?'

What could have gone wrong with the plumbing is exactly the same thing that has gone wrong with the bricklaying, the concrete-mixing, the painting and the roofing (and this is only Page One of a long list). The thing that has gone wrong is that both Fluffy and Ishmael have over-extended their skill sets. 'I think your very special talents lie in other areas,' I tell Fluffy. 'You're more of a people person than a bricks-and-mortar sort of a person.'

Fluffy has made the round trip from hysteria to acceptance and says his talent for dealing with dead people might have a very short lifespan unless he can hire a plumber to come and fix the shower problem asap – Mrs Ho has asked him three times to purchase a knife sharpener. 'She's now at the end of her tether,' Fluffy whimpers.

The other person in my immediate circle who is in a state of mad agitation is Sam Ho, who, after five days of tests, has been diagnosed with twenty-twenty vision and perfect auditory capacity. His brain has also been declared one hundred per cent fit and well and untraumatised by any car accident or incident of domestic assault (the day I broke my toothbrush over his head).

Sam Ho has, however, been told that he has dyslexia. What this means, in layman's terms, is that while he is a very clever boy, with an IQ ten points above Shakira (the singer of the Soccer World Cup official tune has an IQ of 140), he has a learning disability.

Or in the lame-brain language of the mean kids who throng the corridors of Trinity College, Sam Ho is Stupid, Simple and Feeble. Alternatively, to use another six-letter word popular with the fee-paying pedants, Sam Ho is a Retard.

Sam Ho is also still not speaking to me, even when I call him Sam Ho and not Rat Turd, which is the bespoke nickname now bestowed on him by the brain-dead at school. They, who collectively share the intellectually deficient IQ of Britney Spears (104), seem to have trouble remembering Sam Ho's new nickname because they pin it up on the school notice-board next to his photo, post this new information on various popular Facebook sites and, just in case they still can't remember Sam Ho's new nickname, they have given him his own Twitter hashtag (#Ratturdboyattrinitycollege).

Being a bursary girl who knows that dyslexia has absolutely nothing to do with being dumb – in fact the geniuses in the world are members of the Dyslexia Club (ask Albert Einstein and Walt Disney) – I still call him Sam Ho and find it perfectly easy to remember. Sam Ho. Five letters. Like Smart.

The third person in my circle who is in a furious tizz is Fatty. The reason for his agitation: Alistair.

We rendezvous in the park on Saturday afternoon to take stock of our progress. After thirteen phone calls to the SPCA – three each by Melly, Fatty, Sebastian and me (and a last desperate call from Melly) – Alistair remains an abused and miserable dog in the care of Kindness The Caretaker.

Melly says the people at the SPCA are probably really, really busy trying to prevent cruelty to lots of animals. And Alistair is just one small dog among thousands of cruelly treated animals.

Fatty says that Alistair may be a dog in a million tortured dogs, but he is *his* cruelly treated dog, and that makes him one of a kind. 'I just don't know what to do. I just don't know what to do,' he adds, kicking the heck out of the tyre that once served as a seat for the swings.

I tell him to spare the life of the noble tyre and his second-best shoes and isn't it a good thing I'm his home-girl because I know exactly what to do.

'So do I,' Sebastian says. And he gives me a wink that makes my chest close up.

'You do?' asks Melly, looking suspiciously at Sebastian and me.

'We do,' I tell Melly. And for the next half an hour Sebastian and me tell Fatty and Melly exactly what we are going to do to save Alistair.

But because Melly is looking at me with that suspicious face and breathing hard through her nose like an amateur

nose-breather I don't make it easy for her. I tell her she
has to guess first. And I give her clues – crossword style.

The answer to the Sad Alistair Conundrum (SAC) is
the same word for the most populous city in China (eight
across).

Melly looks at me blankly. I'm no mind-reader but I'm
betting fifty yuan that she's wondering how many letters
there are in Beijing. (There are seven.)

I give her another clue. Five down from Clue One:
This action is a simile for the answer to question one and
will require strong nerves. Five letters.

Melly thinks for four minutes. I tell her if she wants
to be a millionaire she can go fifty-fifty or phone a friend.
So she has a whispered consultation with Fatty and he
nods.

'I've got it, April-May,' she says in an accusing voice.
'You want us to *steal* Alistair The Awesome-ist. You want
us to *shanghai* him.'

I grin at Melly. My best friend isn't too stupid. 'Correct.
We are going to kidnap, shanghai, abduct and steal Alistair
and resettle him in a loving home.'

'But that's criminal,' Melly says, doing that annoying
thing with her nose again.

I tell Melly that technically it is not a criminal act.
Sebastian and I have debated this moral point and we
feel comfortable that it is not theft, per se.

'What per se is it, then?' Melly asks.

I tell her that the way Sebastian and me see it is that Alistair technically belongs to Miss Frankel – and not Kindness The Caretaker – so removing Alistair from his care is not an act of theft. In fact, we are simply borrowing him for an indefinite period.

Melly says that I'm on shaky ground, but Fatty silences her with a bony finger. 'Whose ground do I need to shake to get my dog home?' he says.

So I tell him. I outline steps one, two and three that he needs to take this afternoon, ahead of step four (which will see Alistair safe and sound with Fatty in a loving home).

Melly groans and says that it's criminal, but Fatty says that it is what it is and he'll be off then, to take the three steps, and he'll pop by Chez Matchbox in person later to report on progress – and he'll check out the deluxe soccer suite while he's around to see if he can help Fluffy solve the plumbing problem. 'It'll either be late afternoon, or tomorrow, depending on how things work out,' he says.

Melly says that if I don't mind too much she's not coming back to Chez Matchbox with me to play FarmVille on Heaven because she wants to go with Fatty to make sure he doesn't do anything too stupid.

I say that I don't give a soccer jock's smelly socks if she wants to hang out with the criminal element and involve herself in illegal activities. Then I watch her face go pink and sad and wish I could chop my tongue into tiny pieces.

Instead I go back to the park and hang out with Sebastian for a couple of hours. He throws his takkies up into the plane tree to see if they will get stuck and, when they do, he throws my new winter shoes into the plane tree to try and dislodge them. And they get stuck too.

I limp home barefoot to wait for Fatty and his three-step progress report and find Fluffy in a state of heightened hysteria.

'The plumber couldn't come?' I ask him.

Fluffy shakes his head. He opens his mouth but he can't get the words out. Then he says something that sounds like, 'The king is coming to live with us during the Soccer World Cup.'

I ask Fluffy to run this by me again and he says, 'The king. The king of the beautiful game is coming to see us tomorrow about renting the new room.'

'The king? Which king is coming to stay with us?' I ask.

Fluffy becomes even more distraught and garbles on about the player of the century, Manchester United's Number 7, the world's number one striker . . .

I finally get it. Fluffy is saying that some soccer celebrity is going to rent the bedroom and en suite bathroom for the duration of the Soccer World Cup. 'That's weird,' I say. 'I haven't even put the advert on Gumtree yet. I was waiting for you to finish it before I took photographs and posted it via Heaven.'

Fluffy beams at me and says that it really is amazing indeed, and what is the most amazing is that the king seemed to have my cellphone number. 'The king sent us a message on your cellphone. Sam Ho read it to me just ten minutes ago.'

Before I can say 'What the blazes is Sam Ho doing messing with The Brick!' and 'Why can't a girl leave her cellphone at home charging without annoying eight-year-old boys invading her privacy?' I say instead, 'Sam Ho is reading?'

Fluffy nods. 'Just simple things. Slowly. He's trying. It isn't a complicated message.' And then he yells for Sam Ho to bring April's cellphone and read the message from the king.

Sam Ho brings The Brick and clicks on the message.

'Read it, Sam Ho. You can do it,' Fluffy says.

And Sam Ho reads: 'Will come round and check out the posh room and shower tomorrow. Eric Cantona.'

'King Eric. Eric Daniel Pierre Cantona. The finest soccer player the world has ever seen is going to be our very own soccer tourist, staying in the deluxe suite. Can you believe it?' Fluffy says. His eyes are glowing like hot chillis.

I grab The Brick out of Sam Ho's hand and look at the message: *Will come round and check out the posh room and shower tomorrow. Ericcantona.*

I read it and I realise what it means. I read it again and then I turn to Fluffy and say, 'I don't believe it.'

And then I turn to Sam Ho and I hug him. I can't help myself. 'Do you know what you have done, Sam Ho?' I ask him. 'You are the cleverest boy in the whole wide world.'

Sam Ho looks at me with hopeful eyes. 'You think I'm smart, April-May? Really? I'm not a Rat Turd?'

I say that I think that he's not too stupid for a dumb chop who hasn't learned not to mess with my stuff. Not too stupid at all.

Soccer World Cup Update –
Days to Kick-off: 12

Match of the Day –
Fatty *vs* The Odds

Sixteen

King Fatty

'King Eric – Eric Daniel Pierre Cantona, the most awesome soccer player ever to kick a ball – is Ricky's father?' Sebastian asks.

'That means Ricky's half French. King Eric was born in Marseilles, you know – in a cave. No wonder he wants to come and stay here in your nice posh room during the Soccer World Cup,' Melly says.

Melly, Fatty, Sebastian and me are sitting out the back of Chez Matchbox under the sour-sour tree. They came as soon as they could on Sunday morning after I sent them a text message telling them I had some urgent, earth-shattering news.

I tell Melly and Sebastian to slow down. Fast. They're chomping at the wrong end of the stick and getting the facts tangled into a million knots.

'Okay, explain again the earth-shattering news to us. I'm so confused,' Fatty says. His head is in his hands and he is hunched over, trying to make himself as small as possible.

So I tell them the astonishing revelation that came to me as I read the message on The Brick. 'Ricky, I know what your real name actually is.'

Fatty says he actually knows it all too well, and it sucks big time.

I tell him, 'No, it doesn't. Your name isn't Ericca Ntona. It's actually Eric Cantona. You were named after the king.' Fatty's parents either had kinky handwriting, or the person who found him as an abandoned baby and officially recorded his name was not a soccer fan.

'So my name is really Eric, not Ericca – not some silly girly name,' Fatty says. And as he says this the sun moves from behind a cloud and lights up his face. It's sort of gratifying when nature gives a sign that she recognises significant moments.

It was only when Sam Ho read Fatty's cellphone message about coming around to check on Fluffy's dodgy shower that his name was read correctly. For the very first time. Clever, clever Sam Ho.

'So is Eric Cantona his dad or not?' Sebastian asks. 'Is Ricky half French?'

'And is King Eric coming to stay in your posh room?' Melly adds.

I roll my eyes to the gods and give Melly and Sebastian

a drive-through lecture on the physical implications of genetic determination. 'Take a look at him, won't you,' I say, pointing at Fatty. 'I'm betting against it.'

Fatty says he's putting his money with mine. 'I'm so rubbish at soccer. Music is my talent. There's no ways I'm related to the king,' he says.

Then I give Melly and Sebastian a crash course in logic: 'As the text message was actually from Ricky, and not from Eric Cantona, it stands to reason that he's not going to be renting our posh room.'

Expressions of enlightenment wash over Melly and Sebastian's faces, and Melly says she gets it one hundred per cent.

I say that I am glad to hear that we are all reading off the same page now.

Melly says that for sure it's nice to be one hundred per cent correct, but it's not good news, is it? Fluffy must be gutted that the king isn't renting the posh room. I tell her that Fluffy is totally slaughtered and took to his bed last night for the rest of the weekend. But the good news is that we are ten steps closer to finding Fatty's parents.

Fatty sighs and says that I need to take him through this. Slowly. He's struggling to deal with the earth-shattering news.

And so I explain again. Given that Fatty's parents are

160

obviously soccer nuts, there is definitely one place they will be on 11 June.

Sebastian nods. 'Cool, they're going to be renting your posh garage?'

I tell Sebastian that he is a credit to the private school system, but no. The place Fatty's parents will defs be is Soccer City, Soweto, at the opening of the World Cup. And that's where Fatty will find them. Among ninety-five thousand soccer fetishists. Betwixt and between all the people who are crazy enough to name their children Eric Cantona, David Beckham and Lionel Messi.

Fatty says he gets it two hundred per cent. He stands up and nearly takes the top of his head off on a branch of the sour-sour tree. The branch makes an *ouch* noise, which is sort of freaky. 'Of course. I'll find them there. It's my destiny. Just like in *August Rush*,' Fatty says.

August Rush is this movie that Fatty and me have watched seventeen times thanks to Mrs Ho's PVR. It's about a musical child prodigy called Evan who lives in an orphanage and through destiny finds his parents (who are also musicians) at a concert in Central Park. They recognise each other because of their strong love for music. They feel the vibes between them. It's a rubbish movie full of soppy nonsense about mothers and sons and Fatty is addicted to it.

'I'm going to the opening of the World Cup at Soccer

City on 11 June. That's where I'll find them. We will be drawn to each other through our deep love for soccer. The soccer vibes will pull us together like magnets,' Fatty says.

I don't tell Fatty that I know for a fact that his deep love for soccer is about as deep as his love for salad (deeply shallow) – he can't even watch the game on television. I have little faith in the *August Rush* theory of attraction and am still trusting that Rhonda Byrne will come through and make things happen. Or that someone in my country's great child welfare bureaucracy will have the good manners to respond to Sarel The Big Lawyer's increasingly demanding legal letters that I have been emailing weekly from hotcalendargirl, Sarel's legal secretary.

Fatty says that he owes Sam Ho huge. Sam Ho is the boss. He is the bomb and a prince – which means that he is very highly regarded by Fatty. Without Sam Ho he would be walking around with a girl's name for the rest of his life and wouldn't be within twelve days of meeting his real parents. He says that he wants to thank Sam Ho personally and pledge to repay the life debt he owes him. But before he can yell 'Sam Ho', a shrill voice calls from the top of the sour-sour tree: 'I'm here!' And Sam Ho drops to the ground. The little rat-sneak.

Fatty and Sam Ho do some hand-shaking and punching and wrist-tugging to express their new bond of eternal brotherhood, and Fatty says to Sam Ho, 'You gave me my real name back. I totally owe you, brother.'

And Sam Ho says that Fatty won't have to owe him a brother's button if he can help him get *his* name back. 'My name is Sam Ho. Not Rat Turd. I don't like being called Rat Turd at school. It makes me feel worthless and angry.'

Fatty says that he knows exactly how he feels. And maybe this will help. Then Fatty gives Sam Ho the kind of motivational speech that would make Oprah's agents fear for her position as the number one feel-good talk show host on Planet Television.

Fatty tells Sam Ho that ugly names are just something that people who have inferiority complexes give to other people to make them feel better about being losers. The way Sam Ho should see it is that the more times dumb, insecure people call him Rat Turd, the better off he is and the worse off they are. 'They become smaller and meaner by their name-calling, and you become bigger and better for it,' Fatty says, concluding his fifteen-minute Oprah spiel.

Sam Ho asks Fatty if that is the best he can do and Fatty says, 'Sorry, buddy, but you are just going to have to suck it up. It's the consequence of being original.'

I tell Fatty that for sure he's going to make it big on the motivational speaking circuit but right now we have to talk about a certain secret which small trolls can't hear about no matter how original and closely befriended they are to my second-best friend. 'So scoot, Sam Ho.'

Sam Ho says, 'Thanks a bunch, Fatty.'

And Fatty says, 'For the record, my name is Eric, but it's a pleasure, Rat Turd.'

And then they both wipe palms and grin before Sam Ho slouches off in the direction of the couch and the television.

I ask Fatty and Melly to brief Sebastian and me on their activities of the day before, activities which they had embarked upon after leaving the park and which are part of our mission to steal a hairy canine. And then I see Melly's stricken face and say rather, 'I mean our quest to borrow a dog for an indefinite period.'

The day before, Fatty and Melly did reconnaissance. This involved Step One: going to the house next door to Miss Frankel's house and asking to speak to Kindness The Caretaker. Then (Step Two) they went to the house on the other side. And (Step Three) the house across the road. But they never went to Miss Frankel's house to ask to speak to Kindness The Caretaker in case he was actually there. Because they didn't want to speak to him.

By deploying this three-step method of research they managed to establish that Kindness The Caretaker is absent from Miss Frankel's house on weekdays between eight o'clock in the morning and five o'clock at night, when he is employed as a security guard in another neighbourhood. He goes to church at nine o'clock on Saturday mornings, returning home at approximately six o'clock as he is a Seventh-day Adventist. And he is home alone (except for Alistair) all day on Sundays, when he sleeps, plays loud music and does his washing.

They also managed to observe the dividing wall in the back garden that borders Miss Frankel's house and the neighbour on the left-hand side. Melly says this in a smug sort of Harry-casual way. She's waiting for me to ask her how on earth she did that, but I chew on a sour-sour berry and wait for Sebastian to say, 'How on earth did you do that?'

Melly says that he'll never guess in a million years.

Sebastian says that she's right, so perhaps, as time is short, she should just tell him. So she does.

'The person who lives in the house next to Miss Frankel is a teacher from school,' Melly says. 'So when we rang the doorbell and asked to speak to Kindness The Caretaker, he invited us in. And we checked out the back garden and the perimeter when he let his dog out to do her business.'

Melly says that we'll never guess (in a million years) who the teacher is.

'It's Dr Gainsborough,' I say.

She looks at me like I'm a spoilsport, but anyone who

is a fan of maths and logic could have told her that if there are thirty-two teachers at Trinity College and twenty-two of them are female, and of the remaining ten male teachers six of them are juniors who could not afford to own a house in Miss Frankel's 'hood, then of the remaining four teachers, of whom two are sports coaches who play cricket or tennis on Saturday afternoons, this leaves two male teachers. One has a pet and one does not. Duh.

Fatty says that Dr Gainsborough appears to lead a solitary existence. The house betrays no signs of another person and the only photographs (on the mantelpiece in the sitting room) are of animals.

I say that they must be of the three-legged dog called Tripod, and the dog before that, which was deaf from birth, and the cat that couldn't purr.

Melly says that I'm starting to scare her.

I tell Melly that she mustn't get scared until I've told her about Step Four. The step we take to rescue Alistair The Awesome-ist.

Melly says that she can't bear to hear it.

'Listen up,' I reply.

CROSSWORD CLUE 9 [eight across]:
Any long and arduous undertaking or a race in which people run on roads over a distance of 42 kilometres.

Seventeen

The Fourth Step

There are six of us left on the dance floor. It is two o'clock on Saturday afternoon and we have been jigging about for nearly seven hours. My face is dripping with sweat and from the contents of a bottle of water which Melly has shaken out all over me to cool me down. 'Don't give up now, April-May! You can do it, I know you can!' Melly says, leaving my side to go and chuck a bottle of water in Sebastian's face. 'Keep going! Don't stop!' she says to Sebastian. He doesn't skip a beat, throwing his sore leg out to the side to ease the cramps.

Melly tiptoes across the floor to Fatty and gently sprays water over his dripping body. It has the same effect as spraying a buffalo with a perfume dispenser. 'You are the best!' Melly tells Fatty.

Melly has been going around dousing us with water and peppering us with motivational slogans every half-hour for the past seven. She is the sole representative of our support committee and the president of our fan club (it having Melly as its only member).

Fatty, Sebastian and me are among the leftovers from the three thousand and seven entrants to the Eastern Suburbs Catholic Schools Diski Dance Marathon. The prize is two tickets to the opening of the Soccer World Cup, which is happening in six days' time. Between the three of us, we are going to win those tickets and get Fatty to Soccer City to meet his soccer-mad parents. That's the plan.

But Britney, Tiffney, Stephney and someone who looks just like Courtney but isn't – her name is Carol – are the other four remaining contestants, and they are determined that between them they are going to win the prize.

What the Britney Brigade don't realise is that they don't stand a chance because they don't know about Rhonda Byrne and her secret. As I dance I feel the positive vibrations. I imagine myself on the stage, accepting the two tickets from the judges. I am so positive and focused on this outcome that I can feel the two tickets in my hand (even with the three muscle spasms competing with each other in my left calf).

The trick to keeping going is not to lift your feet too high, but to conserve energy by doing a shuffling move along the dance floor. My feet feel like blocks of agony and my legs scream that they need to be amputated at my hips, but I keep focused on the tickets.

169

Sebastian winks at me, but I can see that his gammy legs are taking strain. And Fatty has shed thirteen litres of his body mass onto the dance floor.

Melly also wanted to enter the competition and dance with us. She cried when we told her that she couldn't, but we feared for her patchy lungs. In any case she is essential for team morale, we told her.

I check the clock on the wall and signal to Fatty and Sebastian. The signal means: we gotta go. Fatty signals back: I know we gotta go, but we need to win this first.

'We have to get this done today. It can't wait another week,' I screech above the sound of Shakira and her 'waka waka, this time's for Africa'. Then I look across at Sebastian. He is grimacing in pain. I don't think he's going to last much longer. 'Let's send Sebastian and Melly on ahead. Between you and me we can win this,' I shout at Fatty and he nods in agreement.

The next time Melly comes around to baptise me, I tell her there's been a change of plan. It's down to Sebastian and her to get themselves to Miss Frankel's house and implement Step Four before Kindness The Caretaker gets home from exercising his religious convictions as a Seventh-day Adventist.

It has to be done this weekend. Next Saturday Kindness The Caretaker is going on holiday and taking Alistair back home with him to Mpumalanga for five weeks. Miss

Frankel told Fluffy this when she called to suggest that Alistair board at Chez Matchbox while Kindness went away. 'Not on your life,' Fluffy told her.

In those five weeks Alistair's groove will undoubtedly be crushed once and for all. We need to get him home to Fatty fast.

Melly shakes her head. 'I just can't, April-May. I was going to tell you sooner, but I didn't know how . . .'

'What do you mean you can't?' I stop dancing. 'Ricky and me have to carry on dancing and win. You need to do this. We can't be two places at the same time.'

'Keep dancing! Don't stop!' Melly rasps. If a contestant stops for more than thirty seconds outside of the designated five-minute break each hour then he or she is disqualified. 'I know saving Alistair is the right thing to do, but it's also the wrong thing for me,' Melly says as I shuffle my feet to the music again. 'You're going to think I'm a chicken, but it's not that. I just don't feel comfortable doing this. I'm sorry. Please don't hate me too much.'

I tell Melly that I could never hate her too much. I couldn't hate her even one tiny bit. She's the bravest person I know and she's my best friend forever, no matter what. (Even though she spends more time hanging out with Fatty at the moment and still hasn't given me my big-big birthday present.)

Fatty stumbles over to where we are standing and I tell him Melly doesn't want to play on the dodgy side of the law. 'And Sebastian can't do it on his own.' So it's either him or me.

'You go with Sebastian and I'll keep dancing,' Fatty says. 'I need to win the tickets myself otherwise the vibes won't work. It's what Evan in *August Rush* would do.'

'It's what Evan would do,' Melly affirms.

Since Fatty has learned that his name is Eric (and that the chances of his parents pitching up at the opening of the Soccer World Cup are as certain as the chances of the stiff-mobile getting fertilised by starling droppings each and every day), he has watched *August Rush* twenty-four more times. And Melly has watched the movie with him each and every one of those times. Between them they know exactly how Evan from *August Rush* would behave in any situation. (Except, perhaps, how Evan from *August Rush* would behave if he was saddled with a posh en suite bathroom and no cash-flush soccer fiend to rent it for four weeks – which is the situation Fluffy has found himself in since Eric Cantona blew him off and decided not to come to South Africa after all.)

Sebastian and me stop dancing and walk over to the judge's table and surrender our competition numbers to the jeers of Britney and Tiffney and Stephney and Carol. Then we tell Fatty to keep dancing and Melly to keep him hydrated and Sebastian and me catch a taxi to the scene of the crime.

Step Four of our plan is criminal in its simplicity. We ring the buzzer to the house next to Miss Frankel's. Three minutes later I hear the familiar voice. It doesn't say, 'Who is it?' but, 'Who do you feel you are?'

I tell Dr Gainsborough that it is I, April-May February, his basket case from Trinity College.

Dr Gainsborough buzzes me into his yard and I walk to the front door as Sebastian slinks around to the back of the property.

'You've come about the dream. I just knew it,' Dr Gainsborough says, opening the front door and pulling me into the kitchen.

I keep a wary eye out of the kitchen window, which gives a full view of the back garden that borders Miss Frankel's property, as Dr Gainsborough puts the kettle on. The two houses are separated by a high wall. On the other side of which is the small courtyard otherwise known as Alistair's Prison. Or the Torture Chamber. Anyone standing on the wall in question could easily use a broomstick to open the door to the courtyard, letting Alistair into the front garden, from where he could set himself free under the gate leading to the road.

Dr Gainsborough says that he isn't surprised at all to see me, not after bumping into me in his dream last night.

'Tell me all about it,' I say.

He says that there he was, swimming in a deep river, when he saw a crocodile swimming towards him. But it was a very strange-looking crocodile because it was wearing a pair of sunglasses and a makarapa, which is a peculiar sort of hat soccer supporters wear to big matches.

I say that I know exactly what the crocodile looks like and I am more than familiar with millinery soccer fashions.

'Yes, of course,' Dr Gainsborough says. 'You had the same dream. Which is why you came around.'

I tell him that of course it is, but as I do so I see a mop of golden curls sweep past the kitchen window. I point urgently at something above Dr Gainsborough's head. He looks behind him and up, narrowly missing a waving hand and a head ducking below the window sill. Sebastian is playing silly buggers. If he's not careful, he's going to get caught. I hold thumbs for Rhonda Byrne.

'Yes, I thought you may notice that. My dreamcatcher. I have one in every room.' Dr Gainsborough touches the circle and its long feather tail that dangles from the kitchen cupboard. 'Anyway,' he says, returning to the topic, 'in my dream I see you on the bank of the river and I shout at you to stay right where you are, out of the way of the crocodile, which is swimming towards me.'

Dr Gainsborough then hands me a cup of milky tea and tells me to carry on recalling the dream. He is interested in my perspective. But I tell him that it doesn't happen like that in my dream. 'You see me but you say nothing. You may think you shout a warning, but you don't. You are silent. Instead, you duck under the water and swim for safety. You swim for a long time. It seems to me that you can breathe underwater. You swim away and emerge on the far side of the river. You leave Emily and me on the bank of the river in full view of the crocodile.'

'Emily? My dog Emily?' Dr Gainsborough looks stricken. 'What is she doing there?'

'Yes, she is in the dream. Perhaps you never saw her. And Emily doesn't see the crocodile . . .' I make chopping movements with my hands. Chop, chop, chop.

'But surely, surely she would have smelled the crocodile. She has the keenest sense of smell to compensate for her blindness.' Dr Gainsborough looks around for Emily, as though to reassure himself that she is still with him.

And then there is the sound of barking. 'That's Emily. She's alive,' Dr Gainsborough says, his face breaking out into a smile.

He looks out of the window to where the sound of barking is coming from and I look too. Emily is running around in circles, her teeth bared and her tail wagging as though she is not sure whether she should be fierce or playful.

And then Emily throws herself at the wall. It appears

175

she has decided that fierce is more fun than playful. That is until she throws herself back from the wall and drops a Converse takkie on the grass. Then she sits back and howls.

No, on closer inspection it's not Emily that is howling, it is the forest of bamboo in Dr Gainsborough's garden. The bamboo is howling and thrashing about.

'It seems that my bamboo has become possessed,' Dr Gainsborough says, his eyes gleaming with delight.

I put down my cup of tea and rush out into the garden.

Soccer World Cup Update –
Days to Kick-off: 3

Match of the Day –
The World *vs* April-May

Eighteen

Peekaboo

It has been three days since Sebastian impaled himself on a forest of bamboo after toppling off the dividing wall between Dr Gainsborough and Miss Frankel's properties.

It has also been three days since Alistair The Awesome-ist spotted the open courtyard door – which Sebastian had managed to lever ajar before falling off the wall – and sped off under the gate and down the road to freedom.

And it has been the same three days since Fatty had a chronic asthma attack in the ninth hour of the Eastern Suburbs Catholic Schools Diski Dance Marathon and had to be ambulanced out of the hall – leaving Britney the winner and proud (read smug) owner of two tickets to the opening of the Soccer World Cup.

I have barely survived these three long, miserable days.

I am sitting in my bedroom waiting to be dragged into the kitchen, where the tribal council – Fluffy, Mrs Ho and Mom – are meeting to determine my fate. I stand accused of plotting the attempted theft (and aiding and abetting the subsequent loss) of the beloved canine pet of a valued client-in-waiting of Swallows and Sons (Miss Frankel).

'We'll be about fifteen minutes and then we'll call you and let you know what we have decided,' Fluffy said. But it has been more than an hour and I'm not sure if this is a good or a bad thing.

There is a knock on the door and Sam Ho pokes his annoying face into my private space. I want to tell him to buzz off, but I am in urgent need of some intel. I need to know how the votes are being cast. The ratfink is dying to tell, but I won't ask. I just allow my silence to break him.

'My mom says that she doesn't believe your friend Melly – that it was all her idea in the first place to steal the dog.' Sam Ho swaggers about the room, touching my stuff. He knows I'm not going to chuck him out until he has been bled dry of info. 'And she doesn't believe Eric either – that it was actually his idea.'

A space deep in my tummy shudders and shoots a tingling ball to the back of my throat, making it hard for me to swallow. My best friend and my second-best friend are the silliest, loyalist best friends a person could ever have. They are also rubbish liars. Their attempts to secure me immunity have failed.

'Your dad says that it was probably Sebastian's idea and that he dragged you into it and dragged you down.'

Poor Sebastian. The future butt of every butt joke on Planet World. He is still lying on his stomach in the Milpark Hospital, waiting for a team of nurses to finish extracting bits of bamboo from a place he won't be able to sit down on for the next hundred years.

'I expect the woman to whom I am coincidentally related says that I should be grounded forever and have all means of communication confiscated for the rest of my adolescent lifespan?'

Sam Ho stops mincing about and shakes his head. 'No, your mom says that you behaved the way you did because she raised you capable of choosing between right and wrong and incapable of inertia in the face of evil. She says that she's to blame.'

A hot feeling spreads across my chest and my face feels stiff.

'Oh, and your mom also says that while your intentions were pure, your methods were totally dumb, and that she's not responsible for that part.'

There is a sharp rap on the door and Fluffy sticks his nose inside my room. 'April, we've come to a decision.' The council has cast its vote.

Poor Fluffy is taking strain. Not only has he had Sebastian's parents screaming down the phone at him about bad influences (me), he has also had Miss Frankel threatening legal action against the two thieves and trespassers (Sebastian and me). And on top of this is the cruel knowledge that in three days' time South Africa and Mexico kick off a month of World Cup Soccer and the deluxe suite at Chez Matchbox is still under-occupied (not occupied at all). There has not been a single response to our advert on Gumtree.

Fluffy says that we are in exactly the same position as thousands of other hospitable South Africans who were hoping to throw their homes open to millions of tired and homeless soccer fans. Instead, they have found themselves mortgaged to the last notch on their belts and in danger of being thrown out of their own homes and onto the streets to starve.

And as if this isn't a tough enough cross for Fluffy to stagger about with on his shoulders, there is Mrs Ho, who is being one hundred per cent supportive and sweet and says that she and Fluffy will get through this together. Her sweetness and light is completely unbearable to Fluffy, who knows that he has let her down and wants to rip his toenails off with his teeth and thrash himself senseless.

Fluffy isn't the only one taking things rather badly. I spoke to Fatty briefly on The Brick yesterday. Correction, Fatty did most of the talking and I listened. He was a triple loser, he said. Not only had he lost the opportunity of going to the opening of the Soccer World Cup and finding his parents, he had also lost the awesome-ist dog in the whole world. 'I'm gutted, I don't know how I'll ever get over this,' Fatty croaked, and I heard the sound of a crackling packet.

'What's the third loss?' I asked him, thinking of his poor pal Sebastian lying on his tummy with his lost dignity in hospital.

I heard Fatty catch his breath, like he was holding down a sob (or a mouthful of biscuits). 'Melly's dad won't let her speak to me. I haven't been able to talk to Melly for two days.' His voice faded away and I heard loud chewing. Then Fatty said that he really had to go as he could smell that the lamb-stew was just about ready.

I follow Fluffy into the kitchen and prepare to hear my sentence. It is delivered by Judge Julia Ho, who is not displaying sweetness and understanding towards me. I take my punishment standing up, my eyes fixed on a spot in the middle of Mrs Ho's forehead.

Judge Ho tells me I am to be sentenced to being deprived of Heaven and television for one month – I grab a kitchen chair for support – and, in addition, I must personally apologise to Miss Frankel for seeking to steal her dog (and in the process losing said dog to the streets of Jozi).

'No,' I say before I can swallow my tongue.

'No?' Judge Ho's forehead contracts into a web of lines.

There is a rushing sound in my ears as the blood drains from my face. No Heaven and television for one month? No lovely Mara Louw from M-Net *Idols* or Dr Rey from *Dr. 90210* and his body-conscious babes with boobs like soccer balls? 'I won't apologise,' I say. 'Not today, not tomorrow and not next week. I'm not sorry.'

'That's my girl,' Mom says and touches me on the shoulder.

I sit down as Fluffy starts shredding his hair. 'Well, then I suppose I will have to apologise on your behalf.'

'No, you will not,' says Judge Ho, her forehead contracting even further (into something that would even be a challenge for Dr Rey and his posse of Botox experts).

'No, I will not,' says Fluffy, backtracking. These days he is ready to agree with anything Mrs Ho says to atone for ruining her life and driving our family into despair and bankruptcy and shooting the country's Gini coefficient into the stratosphere. 'So, who will apologise then?'

Mrs Ho says, 'The person sitting at the kitchen table.' Meaning me.

I shake my head. No. I will not.

Mrs Ho, Fluffy and Mom leave me in the kitchen and take the discussion outside the front door for five minutes. On their return they announce payback for my lack of remorse. To consider the consequences of not apologising I am being sent to live with Mom and Sarel in Pretoria for a couple of days. As soon as I decide to say sorry I may return.

My fire has been snuffed out. The tribe has spoken. It's time for me to go.

I spend the next two days with Mom and Sarel in Pretoria until the Peekaboo Party drives me home. The Peekaboo Party is a gathering of one hundred and twenty of Mom's closest girl-friends (and Sarel, who is not a girl), who have come together to drink tea, open presents and view on television the 3D movements of my soon-to-be-born baby brother.

There is a television set in every room of the house and as a nurse scans Mom's tummy with a machine, each heartbeat and movement is beamed to the many screens to 'oohs' and 'aahs' from every room.

Mom says Sarel has taped the scan and is going to try and screen it at the soccer fan parks before the opening of the big game on Friday, just so the whole world can meet his soon-to-be-born son and heir. She says this with a sigh and a tired smile, which I do not see.

At the Peekaboo Party I have to field the question 'Aren't you excited about having a baby brother?' one hundred and twenty times until I am feeling so animated at the thought that I tell Mom that I am taking a taxi straight back to Jozi to apologise to Miss Frankel for trying to steal her dog.

She says, 'Really, May?' And then she says, 'May, you could have come to me with your problem about the dog. Why didn't you just tell me? You can speak to me about anything. Anything at all, you know that?'

I tell Mom I'll be off then and that she mustn't eat too much Peekaboo Cake because her ankles look like they're about to explode.

Before going home I go and hang out in the park, where I practise saying, 'I apologise for trying to steal your dog and then losing it.' Because I really am sorry that Alistair The Awesome-ist is lost and roaming the streets of Jozi cold and scared and all alone. But no matter how hard I test-drive the sentence, the first part just won't come out right. The words get tangled in my vocal cords like some loser wannabe on M-Net *Idols*.

So, instead, I collect some of the things in the park that remind me of Alistair. There is a bit of chewed tyre-seat from the swing, several squished winter bulbs that escaped his voracious appetite and a Kentucky Fried Chicken box.

I set them out on the grass in a circle and I seat myself in the middle, composed in an attitude of focused hope à la Rhonda Byrne. I think positive thoughts about Alistair. I think of him chomping away at Sam Ho's school bag. I think of Alistair and me watching *The Dog Whisperer* together and afterwards saying, 'There's a good boy . . .'

185

and 'Walkies!' to Fluffy. And I think of Alistair gambolling down the pavement towards the park and finding his way home to me.

I fix my mind on Alistair. He is on a cold, dark road and I focus on his furry face. Then I broadcast my positive thoughts into the atmosphere and transmit like a GPS. Turn left. Then right. After five hundred metres turn into the park. 'Come home to me, Alistair The Awesome-ist, come home,' I say.

'Does it work?' a voice as gravelly as a bunch of unwashed spinach asks.

I open my eyes and see a man in a baggy tracksuit staring down at me.

'Who wants to know?' I ask.

The man stretches out his hand and says his name is something a bit foreign and unpronounceable and that he is the soccer coach for a foreign and unpronounceable country. He supposes I have seen him in the newspapers because he is a huge sports celebrity. 'I am just taking some quiet time in the park, away from the paparazzi,' he adds. 'I wander around parks seeking solitude when I am trying to resolve insurmountable problems.'

I don't take his hand because I have been brought up not to shake hands with men in parks, and I tell him that I also like to be alone in parks and now that he is here I am no longer alone.

'Does your magic work – this magic you are performing in your circle? I am in much need of some magic.'

I tell him that of course my magic works in my most upbeat, optimistic and positive voice (just in case Rhonda Byrne is listening). And then I ask him what his insurmountable problem for which he needs magic is?

He says that his problem is that in thirty days he must return home to his unpronounceable country with the Soccer World Cup trophy in his hand luggage. But his team are useless, lazy, unfit, lame-brained and suffering from low morale for some reason, and he needs to inspire them with the confidence to win. 'What is your secret?' he asks me.

So I tell him the secret according to Rhonda Byrne.

'This is indeed magic,' he says when I am done.

I tell the soccer legend that it really is and that I must be going home now. He replies that he's going to spend a few hours in my magic circle, thinking positive thoughts about his useless soccer team, but as a gesture of his appreciation he would like to give a lovely lady a present – the lovely lady being me – and he puts his hand in his pocket.

I tell him that I've been brought up not to accept presents from men in parks with their hands in their pockets. And then I see what he is holding in his hand and I say that I do, though, sometimes accept gifts from soccer legends.

I leave him sitting in my circle, thinking his winning thoughts for his good-for-nothing team, and I positively leap and bounce all the way home, clutching a slice of magic.

I can feel it. It is here. In my hands.

CROSSWORD CLUE 10

[seven down – two words hyphenated]:
A start of an event or activity.

Nineteen

Making the Circle Bigger

Melly, Fatty, Sam Ho and me are squashed like small, salty fish in the back of the stiff-mobile while Fluffy and Mrs Ho wallow in whale-like comfort in the spacious front seats.

It's cold outside, but it is an oven inside. The car's heating is on full blast and Fluffy can't seem to turn it off. It's hot enough to bake pizza.

It is one o'clock on the afternoon of 11 June 2010 and we are on the way to the opening match of the Soccer World Cup, courtesy of the soccer legend with the unpronounceable name who handed me six tickets in the park yesterday.

They are not just any old six tickets. They are front-row tickets. We'll be so close to the field that we'll be able to stick out our legs and trip up the Mexican players as they run past our Bafana Bafana – or so Fluffy claims. That's if we manage to get to Soccer City before the game is over.

The stiff-mobile is stuck in bumper-to-bumper traffic,

which stretches for about twenty kilometres along one side of the road to Soweto. Every ten minutes or so a convoy of black German cars escorted by black-helmeted cops break the speed limit and whisk their VIPs past us down the other side of the road – a lane we could also have been whizzing along if the City Transport savants had not decided to keep it free for the bigwigs.

Sam Ho has done his bit to sandpaper everyone's nerves by blowing his vuvuzela non-stop since we left Chez Matchbox at ten o'clock, but Fatty hasn't said a word. He is as stiff as a corpse with angst.

Melly sits tucked up under his armpit, her tiny hand swallowed up in his tiny hand. 'It's going to be okay, you'll see,' she whispers. 'You'll find them there. Just keep the faith.'

I keep the faith by holding fast to a silver Zakumi doll charm that Melly gave me earlier this morning: 'It's your birthday present. It goes with the bracelet I gave you at the beginning of the year when I left for Cape Town.'

Inscribed on the back of the charm is BFF (Best Friends Forever). And propped up on my bed back home is a life-size Zakumi doll. 'I told you I had a big-big present for you,' she said, adding that she had been waiting for the charm to be inscribed at the jeweller's before giving it to me. She hoped that I'd never thought she'd forgotten. I told her, 'Of course not, best friends never forget.'

Mrs Ho checks her watch again and sighs. 'Is there absolutely nothing we can do, July, to make a bit of progress?' Mrs Ho is no rule-breaker, but being stuck in traffic for the past three hours has made her a bit edgy.

Fluffy says there is definitely something he can do and he moseys out of the traffic into the empty VIP lane. He drives like a demon for several hundred metres, ignoring the crazed hooting of the cars in the slow lane until an army of traffic cops wave him down.

Fluffy leans out of the window. 'I'm sorry, officers, but I have to get to the funeral parlour asap. I have a client in the back who is in danger of creating a severe health hazard if he stays unrefrigerated for much longer – my air con's busted and it's like a furnace in here.'

One cop peers into the car and above our heads to the draped heap in the very back part of the stiff-mobile. He wrinkles his nose and then waves us on down the fast lane.

'My goodness, even I believed you,' Mrs Ho says. She smiles sweetly and tells Fluffy that he is a very creative person and who would have thought that he could say such things with such an innocent face.

Fluffy says, 'Thank you for the compliment.' And then he adds that he just has to make a quick detour to the Swallows and Sons branch in Soweto – to make an urgent client delivery – and then we can be on the road again.

Twenty minutes later a lighter stiff-mobile arrives at

the calabash-shaped stadium along with ninety-five thousand other people who all have to be X-rayed and searched in case we are carrying weapons of mass destruction tucked away in our bags.

Fighter jets scream overhead, the opening ceremony goes by without us and we arrive in our front-row seats just in time to stand up again and sing the national anthem. About sixty thousand people sing with one voice. No – fifty-nine thousand nine hundred and ninety-nine because Fluffy is not singing, he is crying his eyes out. He always bawls like a baby during the anthem. He says that he can't help it. Being a citizen of the world's most beautiful rainbow nation makes him so happy.

For the next half an hour we wave our flags until our arms fall off, we strip our vocal cords screaming, 'Go, Bafana Bafana, go!' and blow our lips swollen on vuvuzelas.

And while we blow and scream and wave, Fatty silently searches the stands, scrutinising each and every face. I ask him what he is looking for in those faces and he says that he can't put a name to what it is, but as soon as he sees it he will know. And as soon as they see his face, they will know. Just like in *August Rush*.

At half-time Fluffy sends Fatty, Melly and me off to buy hot dogs and drinks and Fatty and Melly stand in the hot dog queue while I go in search of sodas. It is as I pass the entrance to a VIP suite that I see them.

I'm just about to hiss 'What are you doing here?' when Mom looks up.

Her face is as pale as a white person's face and her eyes are dark. 'May, what are you doing here?' she gasps. She is walking hunched over, leaning against Sarel, whose face is as pink as a pink person's face gets when he is very stressed out.

I tell Mom that we got tickets to the soccer and that Fluffy has sent Fatty, Melly and me to get hot dogs and drinks, but before I can say much more Sarel grabs me by the arm and says, 'Forget the hot dogs, go get your father, it's an emergency.'

'What sort of an emergency?' I ask and Mom says, 'Here's another one coming!' And she doubles over. The emergency is contractions four minutes apart. 'But you're only due next month,' I say. 'And why do you want Fluffy?'

Sarel goes even pinker and says, 'Your mother and me are VIPs and we came with VIP transport. I need to borrow your father's car to take your mother to the hospital.'

'Please, May, fetch your father,' Mom pleads. I see the panic on her face and I don't argue. I run.

I'm there and back with Fluffy and Mrs Ho and Sam Ho quicker than Sarel can say 'They're three minutes apart now!' Mrs Ho looks at Mom and says, 'Oh dear.' And Mom looks down at her dress and says, 'My waters!'

Her dress is soaked and she's standing in a small puddle.

Sarel looks like he's going to expire from pinkness and Fluffy tells Mrs Ho that he needs to take Mom to the hospital and that she must stay with the young people and make sure Bafana Bafana score that goal. He doesn't know how long he's going to be, but perhaps she can ask Melly or Fatty's parents to get them home after the match. Mrs Ho says, 'Go on, stop dithering!'

Sarel and Fluffy prop up Mom between them and they start hobbling towards the exit. Mom looks behind. She doesn't say anything to me. She doesn't need to. I see something in her face and I go after them, my heart thudding in my shoes.

The journey to the stiff-mobile is undertaken in fits and starts. Sarel has the fits as Mom starts having contractions with increasing frequency. At two minutes apart we finally find our way into the parking lot.

'Where did I park?'

Fluffy looks around for the familiar guano-spattered car and Sarel says, 'Come on, man, we need to get out of here.' Mom's face is glistening with sweat and she's breathing like she's blowing out a million birthday candles one after the other.

Fluffy spots the spattered roof of the stiff-mobile and then he says, 'Oh blow, this is going to be a tight squeeze.' Mom snaps that this is no time for inappropriate jokes, but Fluffy replies that he's not joking. 'Some joker's parked me in.'

It is at this point that Mom groans and says that she really can't bear standing up any more. She crouches down, rests her elbows on her knees and says, 'Please, May, if you could just rub my back. Please.'

Steam starts pouring out of the top of Sarel's frizzy head. 'We're out of time,' he wails. 'We're out of time.' What he means is that they'll never make it to the hospital in Pretoria with the home-birth-from-home facilities and the midwife assisted by a world-class gynecologist. We need a doctor now. And he opens his mouth very wide and shouts: 'I need a doctor. Is there a doctor anywhere?'

But the only reply to his plea is the bellyaching noise made by eighty thousand vuvuzelas. That is until a quiet voice says: 'Somebody is needing me?'

Sarel turns around in shock. 'You are a doctor?'

The parking attendant says that this is exactly what his mother called him when he was born thirty-five years ago, and she calls him the same to this very day. He is Doctor Specialist Professor Moyo from Zimbabwe. Then he looks down and sees Mom squatting in the parking lot, panting like an oxygen-deprived guppy. 'I see why you require my services,' Doctor Specialist Professor Moyo says.

Sarel loses his head at this point. It shoots off his neck like a cork out of a bottle of champagne. He starts grabbing at the tufts of hair on his head and then covers his eyes with both hands and jumps up and down.

When he recovers his head Sarel kneels down next to Mom. 'Babe, we aren't going to make it to hospital,' he says. 'We need to operationalise Plan B.'

'What's Plan B?' Fluffy asks.

And Mom says, 'Sarel, Plan B? We never talked about a Plan B?'

'It's where we have the home birth-from-home without the midwife and the world-class gynae and all the equipment I wanted to plug you into,' Sarel says miserably.

I stop rubbing Mom's back as I hear footsteps skidding across the parking lot. The face of an annoying troll-child appears. Sam Ho is flushed and panting. 'I've got a doctor and a nurse for you,' he says. 'They're part of the Soccer World Cup Medical Services Support Team. The best in the world.'

A man and a woman dressed in brilliant-white outfits appear behind Sam Ho. The woman is Dr Stella and the man is Nurse Bradley.

I tell Sam Ho that he's a star for finding help by reading *Soccer World Cup Medical Services Support Team* on the medical suite door. And Sam Ho says that there was a big red cross on the door, so he didn't have to read anything, but here they are anyway.

Sarel looks at Sam Ho as if he could kiss him. Instead

he grabs Mom and kisses her. She pushes him away. 'Oh don't, please, don't touch me.' And then she gives a really loud moan.

Fluffy makes a scared face. 'Oh, I know those signs, she didn't want me in the same country as her when her time came.'

Dr Stella and Nurse Bradley say they don't like the look of Mom one little bit. She hasn't torn a hamstring or ripped a tendon in her ankle. Neither is she in a life-threatening coma (something that certain players are prone to when they want to get off the field and away from their supporters pronto after failing to score the winning goal).

'She's going to have a baby,' Sarel says.

Dr Stella says that she can see that and she wishes she could help but she never really went very deeply into delivering babies when she was studying sports medicine. 'Me neither,' Nurse Bradley says. He's handy at cold packs and bedpans and can go to a splint at a push. 'Sadly, this situation is way outside my speciality,' he says (mournfully).

Doctor Specialist Professor Moyo steps forward and says that as a trained gynaecologist from the University of Cape Town this is indeed his speciality. He has a bona fide degree proving his qualifications that he purchased from a Nigerian colleague working the parking lot across the road. And if his two medical colleagues would just hand him a pair of sterile gloves and secure him some boiled water he'll get on with things then.

Mom allows me to lead her to the back of the stiff-mobile. And then she asks me to hold her hands and, 'Please, May, don't let go.'

I don't let go. Not once. Even when the stadium erupts with screams of joy in the fifty-fifth minute as Siphiwe Tshabalala scores the first goal in the Soccer World Cup for South Africa, I don't let go.

Soccer World Cup Update –
Days to Kick-off: -3

Match of the Day –
April-May *vs* Mom *(replay)*

Twenty

The Visitors

We are receiving visitors today. Fluffy, Mrs Ho, Sam Ho and me.

Mrs Ho has laid out her special visitors' tea set and has bought six dozen koeksisters from a relative of Ishmael's (whose son's aunty works in the catering business).

I have interned a couple of two-litre Cokes in the fridge for my guests and have secured promises from Mrs Ho of the leftover koeksisters once her guests have guzzled to a state of elegant sufficiency.

The first visitor to arrive is Miss Frankel. She is the guest of Fluffy and Mrs Ho and so she gets offered a special cup of tea and a plate of fried syrupy dough – and not a glass of Coke.

After Miss Frankel is settled with snack on couch (brushed hairless and de-ponged by a wipe-down with industrial-strength fabric cleaner) she gives me a look which says that it's time for you to grovel – or pretend to grovel, which is the way I am viewing the exercise.

I have not yet made up my mind whether I am going to speak lies or truth to power, so I compromise and do both. 'I'm sorry I tried to steal your dog, and I'm sorry I got him lost,' I tell Miss Frankel. I say the last part of the sentence very loudly and slowly and the first part fast and soft. Because I'm only sorry about the second part.

Miss Frankel sniffs at me and says, 'Why did you do it? Why did you steal my dog? That dog was my life.'

I tell her that I did it because Alistair was being ill-treated by her unkind caretaker.

'Who's Alistair?' she asks.

I tell her that Alistair was her life.

'Oh, is that what he was called,' she says.

Fluffy and Mrs Ho are hovering in the doorway and I can detect from their body language (arms wrapped all the way around their bodies and legs criss-crossing at the ankle) that they do not believe my meeting to apologise to Miss Frankel is going very well.

'I'm going to get your life back,' I say. 'I've made sure that Alistair will be home soon.' I don't tell her about Rhonda Byrne and the secret ceremony I did in the park because she doesn't look the type to keep faith with mumbo-jumbo like this. But I do hold thumbs behind my back and send a virtual message to Rhonda to please hurry as we are running out of time. And then I rub the Zakumi charm on my bracelet. It's something Melly would do.

Miss Frankel sniffs again (like she doesn't believe me and not like she has the flu) and says, 'How soon? When will I have my darling creature back?'

I feel a smelly, slobbery face chomping at my hand and I say, 'Like, five seconds ago.'

Alistair leaps onto the couch and starts growling at Miss Frankel. The noises he is making are get-off-my-couch-you-miserable-old-witch-who-was-too-mean-to-invest-in-a-pool-net-so-that-my-family-drowned-and-I-got-cruelly-orphaned-and-then-abandoned-and-tortured. He then gobbles up her koeksisters.

Before I can shout 'Alistair where have you come from, you awesome-ist dog', Fatty and Melly walk into the house – followed by Dr Gainsborough and Emily, trotting blindly at his ankles. It appears that Dr Gainsborough has brought Alistair home.

Fatty and Alistair get involved in some serious reunioning – licking and patting and rolling about – while Dr Gainsborough introduces himself and Emily to Fluffy, who he has never met, but not to Mrs Ho, who they (or at least Dr Gainsborough but not Emily) see every day at school and with whom they are both fully acquainted.

Dr Gainsborough says that he has quite the story to tell about how Alistair came into his possession. Everyone focuses their attention on him and waits patiently for him to tell the dramatic tale of how he found and saved Miss Frankel's beloved dog from the cruel and hungry streets of Jozi.

He says that Emily sensed Alistair hanging about outside his house yesterday. He pats Emily on the head. 'An extraordinary thing, for a blind dog to be able to sense another dog a couple of metres from her specially marked territory.' And he gives Emily another congratulatory pat on the head for being so clever and alert.

They lured Alistair onto the property with the aid of a packet of Marie biscuits and gave him refuge and sustenance overnight. He says Alistair appears to have a mighty appetite and following a midnight footwear feeding frenzy he is now down to a pair of slip-slops.

They are now returning Alistair to his safe space (the first home he had after his traumatic loss as a puppy) – Dr Gainsborough continues – until he can be reunited with Miss Frankel.

The good doctor's eyes light up when he sees the owner in question, cowering on the couch, peering at Alistair from behind her fringe of hair. They have been neighbours for fifteen years, but have never met.

Miss Frankel declines Dr Gainsborough's outstretched hand, and continues cowering on the couch. Dr Gains-borough's eyes brighten further. His finely tuned extra-special sixth sense, which allows him to zone in on psychologically needy people, is working overtime. He sits down on the couch and tells her to speak to him. She can tell him everything. So she does.

Miss Frankel has spent the past fifty years of her life loving her animals. 'They are my life. My only connection with this world, Mr Gainsborough,' she says.

Dr Gainsborough nods. How strange, he feels the same. 'And you can call me Doctor, if you would prefer. Or Siggy . . .' – a nickname he would like to be called if he was ever close enough to another person to have a nickname.

'But now, Doctor Siggy,' Miss Frankel continues, 'I can't look at Alistair, or any other animal for that matter.' She is wracked with guilt. If only she hadn't been such a tight-fisted old witch and had spent some cash on a pool net, she would not have lost her beloved family. She is all alone now, crippled by remorse and stony broke. 'My house is mortgaged to the hilt. The bank is banging at my door, and soon I will have no place to lay my head. And no one to love.'

The song sounds familiar – it's the one Fluffy's been singing all week.

Dr Gainsborough says that Miss Frankel should see this as the first of many healing conversations, and Fatty, Melly and me leave Dr Gainsborough and Miss Frankel connecting about their disconnected status on the couch.

We go and liberate the Coke from the fridge and a few sticky koeksisters from the Tupperwares which Mrs Ho has hidden in the chipped-mug cupboard.

We sit outside under the sour-sour tree with Alistair, who has decapitated Sam Ho's vuvuzela and is fertilising the flower beds with bits of green plastic.

'So, what is she like?' I say.

Fatty looks down at his small hands with the toothpaste-white fingernails and doesn't answer. He knows who I'm talking about – the mother he found at Soccer City three days ago – so I wait, allowing the silence to nudge him into a response.

'She loves me more than anything else in the whole wide world.' Fatty gives me a nod when he says this. He knows I know what this kind of love means.

I get a hot feeling across my chest as Fatty's face glows. I want to hear more about his mother. 'Go on. Go on.'

'She's there for me, a million per cent. She says I'm the son she's always wanted from the very moment she ever thought about having a child.'

I feel happy for Fatty. I really do. But I want to howl, for reasons that I don't like to dwell on too much, which may or may not have something to do with my own mother. I eat a koeksister instead and let Alistair lick my fingers.

I ask Fatty how he found her among all those people at Soccer City.

'She found me, April-May. She came to get me and picked me out from the crowd.'

I tell Fatty that's totally gangsta and that I can't wait to meet her.

Fatty passes Melly his koeksister because he says that he just doesn't feel so hungry any more, and as he does a look passes between them.

'Tell her, why don't you?' Melly whispers to Fatty.

And Fatty says, 'She'll figure it out, Mell-Bell. She needs to.'

Before I can tell them that it's not fair keeping secrets from your best friend, Melly asks me when Mom is arriving. She asks it very carefully, in case I explode. Because Mom will soon be arriving with Sarel. And with Siphiwe Tshabalala – the rainbow nation's number one citizen, and hero for life, who scored the very first goal of the Soccer World Cup.

And attached to this hysterically happy threesome will be the world's paparazzi, who have come to photograph Siphiwe Tshabalala with his miniature namesake, who was born in the fifty-fifth minute of the opening match at Soccer City – my new sibling.

Mom is hoping to persuade me to be part of the photo opportunity. But I don't think so.

'This is them now,' I tell Melly as the tornado descends.

The next thirteen minutes at Chez Matchbox are

recorded in a whirlwind of digital photographs which are transmitted from one end of Planet Media to the other and which appear on every front page of every newspaper and website in the universe.

There they are, for the whole world and their dog to see (sorry, Emily): Mom, Sarel, a blob in a receiving blanket (the famous sibling), Doctor Specialist Professor Moyo and Alistair (Alistair making his mark on the ball used to score the famous goal). I am not in this photograph. Neither is Siphiwe Tshabalala, because although he was supposed to be in attendance he is very hot property and is doing a photo shoot for an international sports magazine. But he sent the ball and presents for the baby with his agent.

When the world's paparazzi leave, having snaffled every last crumb of the koeksisters and flattened Mrs Ho's winter seedlings, Mom comes outside. She asks Fatty and Melly if they would be so kind as to go and help Mrs Ho wash the tea things and to help Sarel find the right end of the baby's nappy.

Then she sits down next to me under the sour-sour tree.

I get up.

Mom says, 'May, sit down, I want to talk to you. And I want you to listen. Please.'

I start walking away, and then I look down and see

208

my bracelet with the little Zakumi charm: What Would Melly Do?

I know what my Best Friend Forever Melly would do. She would let Mom talk. And she would listen.

So, instead, I yell at Mom. I yell out all the things that I've kept buried in a hard space at the bottom of my tummy. All the things I haven't been thinking about for the past six months since I read her old diary: 'You never wanted me. You got pregnant before you and Fluffy got married and you didn't want to have me. You wrote it all in your diary. I read it all.'

There. I said it.

Then, as it all drains out of me, I sit down next to Mom. I let her talk and I listen.

Mom tells me that what I say is one hundred per cent true. But no matter how she felt when she was young and scared and first found out she was having a baby, from the moment I was born, from the moment she held me in her arms, she loved me more than anything else in the whole wide world. 'May, your father and me loved each other. We started out a bit differently to lots of other parents, but we loved each other. And we loved you. Nothing can take that away.'

I want to believe Mom – that she never thought about dumping me in a locker room with a dumb name scrawled on a piece of paper tied around my ankle. I want to trust that she never even thought about having that thought. I tell her that I feel confused. I get up and go inside to find Fatty and Melly. Mom follows me, but I pretend she isn't there.

Melly says that Fatty's outside, waiting for his mom, and I say, 'Good, I want to meet her.'

'I want to meet her too,' Mom adds.

Fatty walks up the pavement towards us. I recognise the pale-faced woman next to him – the woman called Grace who adopted him a year ago. And I don't know what to think any more.

Fatty says he wants to introduce his mom to my mom. And he does. She says, 'Grace.'

And Mom says, 'Glorette.' And then they shake hands.

And while they are chatting about the sorts of stuff that moms chat about when they first meet one another I take Fatty aside. 'I don't understand,' I hiss. 'Where's your real mom, the one you went to Soccer City to find?'

Fatty shakes his head at me and says that all that *August Rush* stuff is just Hollywood rubbish. This is real life. He says that his real mom was probably a nice lady who had big dreams for him but who ran out of hope. Maybe one day he'll meet her, and maybe he won't, but in the meantime he's got a mom who loves him more than anything else in the whole wide world. 'I'm lucky, just like you, April-May,' he says.

I tell Fatty that I really don't get it. 'You wanted to meet your real mom so much. What changed?'

'Everything,' Fatty says. 'There was no one there for me at Soccer City, April-May, no one. As much as I looked, they weren't there.' Fatty grabs me by the shoulder and grips me hard with that small hand of his. His voice crackles. 'And then she was there. She came to fetch us after the game, and I saw her there, waving and smiling at me in the crowd.'

'Grace? She came to fetch you?' I say.

'Yes, and when I saw her it all kind of fell into place. She had chosen me, April-May. Out of all of those kids in the orphanage. She chose me.'

'Of course she did,' I say to Fatty.

His hand grips me harder. So hard I want to say, 'Hey, you're hurting me.'

'And your mom chose you, April-May,' he goes on. 'She chose to have you. When she was young and scared and wanted to run away. Just like my mom, but different.'

I tell Fatty that this is true. We look across at our moms and they are laughing about something. They look at us.

I hear a baby crying. I tell Mom somebody needs us. And together we go inside.

The Eight Photographs

There are seven other photographs that were taken the day Siphiwe Tshabalala never came to Chez Matchbox for his photo shoot with the miracle baby of Soccer City (my sibling). These photos didn't make it onto the front pages of the world's newspapers and Internet sites, but they made it onto my Facebook page in an album called: *The Day Siphiwe Tshabalala Almost Came To Visit*.

There's the photo of Fatty, his mom and Alistair The Awesome-ist in their red Toyota Corolla off home after that eventful visit. Miss Frankel agreed that Alistair would be happiest living with Fatty while she worked through her guilt issues with Dr Gainsborough. And that it would take at least twenty years.

The next photo is of annoying troll-boy Sam Ho in soccer legend Siphiwe Tshabalala's Number 8 soccer jersey, which he gifted to Sam Ho. Siphiwe (or his agent) has written for Sam Ho to read (or not to read): *For my buddy*

Sam Ho, who is da bomb – your pal, Siphiwe Tshabalala.
This memento may or may not ease the pain for Rat Turd
during the mean days to come at Trinity College.

The third photo is of Chez Matchbox's deluxe suite.
You can see the South African flag on all four walls and
on the curtains and carpet and moisturiser dispenser. I
have put it in my Facebook album to show all those seven
thousand dribbling would-be tenants who applied the day
after they saw Siphiwe Tshabalala's agent kicking the
winning ball across the room what they are missing. You
snooze you lose, pals. We got ourselves our Eurotrash
soccer-nut tenant all the way from Cape Town.

The fourth photo is of my dad Fluffy and his special
lady Julia Ho having a koeksister moment out back under
the sour-sour tree when they thought no one was looking.
Yes, it's gross, what else can I say?

The fifth photo is of Dr Gainsborough and Miss Frankel
on the couch. Dr Gainsborough looks like he has found
the patient from heaven. Miss Frankel looks like she's
found someone to be patient with. They don't look like
they will be moving from the couch, ever. I just hope that
when they are over connecting they will remember to feed
Emily.

The sixth photo is of Sebastian. He wasn't at Chez
Matchbox the day Siphiwe Tshabalala almost came to
visit, but I put a photo in anyway, because although

213

everyone wants to keep us apart, I think he belongs in this album with me.

The seventh photo is the one I like most of all because it's of Mom, my baby sister and me. Yes, my baby sister. The gods and Rhonda Byrne heard me. Mom says that she's hit the jackpot twice. She now has two daughters.

Sarel says his daughter is the most beautiful girl in the world – next to her mother and his other daughter (me). We have called her June Siphiwe Tshabalala. She'll have to learn to suck it up. I'll help her.

And then there's the eighth photo. It's not in the album on my Facebook page. In fact, it hasn't been taken. It's the one that lives on with the ending to the eighth story and into the beginning of the next. It's the photo of Melly, Fatty and me.

Acknowledgements

I would like to thank Hot Key for giving April-May and me a home and doing what they do so brilliantly; Tina Betts, James Woodhouse and Reneé Naude for helping to make this book happen; and Mike, Emily, Sophie and Jack for everything else that matters.

Edyth Bulbring

Edyth Bulbring was born in Boksburg, South Africa and grew up in Port Elizabeth. She attended the University of Cape Town where she completed a BA whilst editing the university newspaper *Varsity*. Having worked as a journalist for fifteen years, including time spent as the political correspondent at the *Sunday Times* of South Africa covering the first ever democratic elections, Edyth moved into writing full time. Edyth has published six books in South Africa. *100 Days of April-May* is the sequel to *A Month with April-May* and these are the first of her books to be published in the UK.